Moving Bodies

by Arthur Giron

A SAMUEL FRENCH ACTING EDITION

SAMUEL
FRENCH
FOUNDED 1830

NEW YORK HOLLYWOOD LONDON TORONTO

SAMUELFRENCH.COM

ISBN 978-0-573-69742-5   Printed in U.S.A.   #29185

MUSIC USE NOTE

Licensees are solely responsible for obtaining formal written permission from copyright owners to use copyrighted music in the performance of this play and are strongly cautioned to do so. If no such permission is obtained by the licensee, then the licensee must use only original music that the licensee owns and controls. Licensees are solely responsible and liable for all music clearances and shall indemnify the copyright owners of the play and their licensing agent, Samuel French, Inc., against any costs, expenses, losses and liabilities arising from the use of music by licensees.

IMPORTANT BILLING AND CREDIT REQUIREMENTS

All producers of *MOVING BODIES* must give credit to the Author of the Play in all programs distributed in connection with performances of the Play, and in all instances in which the title of the Play appears for the purposes of advertising, publicizing or otherwise exploiting the Play and/or a production. The name of the Author *must* appear on a separate line on which no other name appears, immediately following the title and *must* appear in size of type not less than fifty percent of the size of the title type.

MOVING BODIES was first produced as part of the Ensemble Studio Theatre's second annual First Light Festival in New York City on April 10, 2000. The production was presented by the Alfred P. Sloan Foundation and the Ensemble Studio Theater (Curt Dempster, artistic director; M. Edgar Rosenblum, executive director; Jamie Richards, executive producer) The performance was directed by Chris Smith, with sets by Kert Lundell, costumes by Chris Peterson, lighting by Greg MacPherson, and sound design by Robert Gould. The production stage manager was Jim Ring, the assistant director was Heather Ondersma, and the associate producers were Maria Gabriele and Eileen Myers. The cast was as follows:

RICHARD FEYNMAN	Chris Ceraso
MEL FEYNMAN	William Wise
LUCILLE FEYNMAN	Polly Adams
JOAN FEYNMAN	Amy Love
FRANKY	Kurt Sinnamon
SALLY RAND	Julie Leedes
JULIUS LOWENTHAL	Peter Hermann
ARLENE GREENBAUM	Tracy Sallows
ROBERT OPPENHEIMER	Robert Boardman
CHAIRMAN	David Teschendorf

MOVING BODIES was produced by the L.A. Theatre Works in 2008, and subsequently recorded for L.A. Theatre Works' Audio Theatre Collection. It was directed by Rosalind Ayres. The producing director was Susan Albert Loewenberg and the recording engineer/sound designer/editor was Mark Holden. The cast was as follows:

YOUNG RICHARD FEYNMAN	Alec Medlock
RICHARD FEYNMAN	Alfred Molina
MEL FEYNMAN	Mark Halerik
LUCILLE FEYNMAN	Jenny O'Hara
YOUNG JOAN FEYNMAN	Mary McGowan
JOAN FEYNMAN	Kathryn Hahn
FRANKY	Matt Gaydos
SALLY RAND	Jessica Chastain
JULIUS LOWENTHAL	Harry Groener
ARLENE GREENBAUM	Emily Bergl
ROBERT OPPENHEIMER	Raphael Sbarge
CHAIRMAN	John Vickery
GWYNETH	Jill Gascoine
RABBI	Arye Gross
DORIS	Katharine Leonard
MR. GRAHAM	Joe Spano

CHARACTERS

Richard Feynman
Mel Feynman
Lucille Feynman
Joan Feynman
Franky
Sally Rand
Julius Lowenthal
Arline Greenbaum
Robert Oppenheimer
Chairman

ACT ONE

(Washington, D.C., February 10, 1986. The Challenger Inquiry Commission is in session. What caused the Shuttle to explode? Staring at a handsome, tall model of the Challenger Shuttle is RICHARD "DICK" FEYNMAN in middle age. DICK wears glasses, which he removes when he relives the years of his youth and slips back on when he returns to the present. In a spotlight, as he studies the orange and white model, in his mind he hears Chopin piano music and recalls a news broadcast eyewitness report of the Challenger explosion.)

VOICE OF NEWSMAN. We have a report from the flight dynamics officer that the vehicle has exploded.

(In silhouette, PEOPLE from RICHARD's past watch him. They could be members of the Commission. As audience members could be as well. RICHARD addresses his words to them.)

DICK. I remember my sister and I gawking in wonder at a model of the space ship of the future at the Chicago World's Fair. A young guy in a Flash Gordon space suit was taking signatures from kids who wanted to sign up to be the pilots of the future. My sister asked if she could get hurt if she climbed aboard. He said the government could be trusted never to hurt anyone...because a manned space craft would never lift off its launching pad until all the proper tests had been performed.

(DICK's father, MELVILLE FEYNMAN, appears. A sharp dresser, he is a well-read charmer.)

MEL. Champ, when we get to the Chicago World's Fair you're going to be so inspired by advances created by men got big, hot imaginations like you. WAM! PAM! BAMB! Rockets! Space ships! Champ, you're going to feel like a kid in a candy store!

*(**DICK**'s mother, **LUCILLE** appears. Little sister **JOAN** beside her. **DICK**, 15 years-old, drives a new 1933 Oldsmobile. The family is extremely attractive. The men speak with a slight Brooklyn accent. A banner on the roof of the car reads "1933 Chicago World's Fair or Bust!")*

LUCILLE. No eating candy between meals.

MEL. Champ, women don't have brains for abstract thinking.

DICK. I'd trade my math trophies to swat one home run. So don't call me Champ 'cause I ain't one.

JOAN. I'd trade my piano for a telescope.

LUCILLE. You heard your father, girls aren't born with brains for science.

DICK. Zooommm!

LUCILLE. Stop speeding!

*(**MEL** hands her a pair of binoculars.)*

MEL. Lucille, keep your eyes peeled for cops. Flash Gordon doesn't have a license.

DICK. How am I doin'? Zooooom –

LUCILLE. We're going to crash.

MEL. I'm watchin' him like a hawk.

DICK. Holy Toledo! Pop, look at those birds wrestlin' in midair! Never seen two birds stuck together like that, wings flappin'. Must be a boy and a girl bird makin' whoopie in midair! Wow! Let's see what the Encyclopedia Britannica says.

MEL. Lucille pass me the "B" volume.

LUCILLE. These books are tearing my stockings.

*(**MEL** starts thumbing through pages.)*

MEL. Ritty, I really love it when you notice things.

LUCILLE. Breathe the country air children.

JOAN. I'm breathing.

LUCILLE. Ritty, are you breathing?

DICK. Mama! I can't breathe and drive at the same time.

MEL. Here we go: Birds. What do you want to know? Migratory stuff....

DICK. How come feathers give me a charge?

MEL. Forget about it. Sex and science don't mix. A law of life.

DICK. Explain.

MEL. Son, scientists are like monks. No dames. I would have been content to wash bottles in a lab someplace, but I took one look at your Mama and BAM – CRASH – CRUNCH! Off the path.

DICK. Read to me about that.

MEL. Let's stick with the "B" book.

DICK. Okay. Look up: Boy. Brain. Body.

MEL. What do you want to know?

DICK. When's my body gonna catch up with my brain?

JOAN. DOG! That makes one hundred and fifty since we left Far Rockaway. I'm way ahead.

LUCILLE. Look – hay! Every time you see hay in bundles make a wish.

MEL. Superstition.

LUCILLE. Joan, honey, what did you wish for?

JOAN. I told you already.

LUCILLE. Change it. We don't chew bacon.

JOAN. I got money in my hanky to buy bacon in Chicago.

LUCILLE. Where'd you get it?

DICK. Don't tell.

JOAN. It was a scientific experiment. Ritty paid me four cents.

MEL. To do what, Sugar?

JOAN. Stick my finger in an electric socket.

LUCILLE. What happened?

JOAN. I got electrocuted.

LUCILLE. Mel! Hit the driver.

DICK. CAT! *I* got fifty cats and a hundred and twenty dogs.

JOAN. COW!

DICK. Cows don't count.

JOAN. Stands to reason when you leave New York, what are you going to find out here?

MEL. Hobos. I've counted about three hundred. Ritty, you're goin' to end up a bum if you don't keep your grades up and stop thinkin' about dames. A good number cruncher like you could end up in a big company keepin' the books.

LUCILLE. The highest calling in America today is to be a comedian. Children, who keeps us from being blue?

DICK & JOAN. Groucho, Fred and Jack.

MEL. He's not goin' to be on radio. He's goin' to be an accountant.

JOAN. Can't he grow up to be a funny accountant?

DICK. I thought you said that if you had a boy, he'd grow up to be a scientist.

MEL. Yeah. A happy scientist on the side, like me. But these are hard times, who knows how a scientist gets a salary? I don't.

DICK. Can't you make money in this country doing somethin' you love?

MEL. No. A law of life in America.

LUCILLE. What did Jack the Ripper's mother say to her son?

DICK. How come you never go out with the same girl twice?

(*laughter*)

Hey, Lady. Is your husband hard to please?

LUCILLE. I don't know. I never tried.

(*laughter*)

Ritty, summers why don't you work in the kitchen at one of those big hotels in the Catskills and tell jokes. That would be a lot better than going off into the woods with your father when he comes up weekends. What do you two boys do? Fill your pockets with fossils, feathers. Nature gets men dirty.

JOAN. A motorcycle cop is coming!

LUCILLE. MEL! He doesn't have a license! Be a father for once. If you don't take the wheel, the boy's going to end up behind bars!

DICK. My tummy's startin' to turn over from the arguing.

JOAN. Yuck.

LUCILLE. Hush. Your brother's got a delicate constitution.

DICK. I AIN'T DELICATE!

(A police siren. DICK parks. FRANKY, a young motor-cycle cop, strides to DICK. Takes out pad. DICK stares straight ahead, motionless.)

FRANKY. *(tough)* What seems to be the trouble here?

JOAN. We're goin' to the Chicago World's Fair or Bust.

MEL. To the Hall a Science to be precise!

JOAN. The driver's a scientist. He makes sparks fly in his room.

FRANKY. New York license plates...Jews, huh? Okay, Mr. Einstein, hand over your driver's license. Okay, out of the car. All of you.

(They all get out. He looks inside the car.)

Transporting any booze? What a mess. You people live like gypsies. Never seen such a suspicious crew. Open the trunk.

MEL. Who's got the key? Ritty packed the car.

JOAN. My brother, the driver, can pick the lock.

FRANKY. Oh, yeah? He got priors?

MEL. It's perfectly innocent. A magician came to our town, an escape artist. I paid him to teach us how he does it and my son – who loves to solve puzzles – became an enthusiast. Now he wants to try safecracking.

FRANKY. If the punk's a scientist, how come he ain't wearing a white jacket?

MEL. I'm in the uniform business. I'd be honored to fit you out with a new uniform, gold buttons. No charge.

(**FRANKY** *pulls gun out of his holster, points it at* **DICK**.)

FRANKY. Thinking of knocking over some banks? I'm waiting. Prove you're a real scientist or else! Open the trunk.

DICK. No.

FRANKY. I'm taking you in. And I'm impounding the car.

(*Starts to put handcuffs on* **DICK**, *whose Brooklyn accent becomes more pronounced when he feels vulnerable.*)

DICK. *(tough)* What's ya name?

FRANKY. Franky.

DICK. Mine's Dick. Shake.

FRANKY. No.

DICK. Rub ya hands together.

FRANKY. No.

DICK. I just want to show ya a scientific principle. Come on, rub ya mits together.

FRANKY. No.

DICK. Then *I'll* participate in this little experiment with ya. I'm goin' to rub my hand over yours. Don't be a chicken.

(*He grabs* **FRANKY**'s *hand, rubs his hand vigorously*)

Your hand got warm, didn't it?

FRANKY. Yeah.

DICK. You know why? Friction.

FRANKY. Friction?

DICK. Friction makes heat because ya hand is made outta atoms.

FRANKY. Atoms?

DICK. Atoms can do anything animals can do. Only they're very small. Like when you're lying on the grass, and stare into it –

FRANKY. You begin seeing little things living in there, moving.

DICK. Good, very good. Only atoms are much smaller.

FRANKY. So why did my hand turn warm?

DICK. Brother, ya got piles a atoms in ya hand and when ya push'em against each other ya bump de atoms together and it shakes'em, and de remainin' shakin' motion dat's left when you take dem apart, dat's de warmth ya feel.

FRANKY. Stop dancing around.

DICK. I'm catchin' fire! We're used ta hot and cold, but de only difference between 'em is de speed dat de atoms are jigglin' – dey jiggle more and it corresponds to hotter. And colder is jigglin' less. So, if ya got a bunch a atoms de heat spreads by mere contact. Atoms are always jigglin' like moving bodies. And their jigglin' passes their motion onta others. Atoms attract each other – dey like to be next to each other, dey want as many partners as dey can get.

FRANKY. I understood your funny talk. I used to have a chemistry set. Maybe I could understand other things. No. My Dad don't like me to get above myself. He says I'm safe working for the state. He worries I could become a hobo.

DICK. My old man worries about the same thing.

FRANKY. I guess you people ain't so different from us.

DICK. Reason I didn't want ta open the trunk is it's full a toilet paper, blankets, pots and pans. Because we're Jews, we couldn't stay in some boarding houses. Lots a diners "restricted," too.

FRANKY. Guess that's why you live like gypsies.

DICK. Come live with us and see what life in a Jewish family is like. It's fun. We've always got stuff going on. Tryin' to learn the "Why" of things. Penetrate, deep into mysterious stuff. My Pop's got the biggest science library on the planet. Mom, can Franky come live with us?

MEL. Officer, why don't you come along with us to the fair? You could show us the way.

FRANKY. Sir, it would give me the greatest pleasure.

(He exits. **THE FAMILY** *gets back in the car. Crossfade. Sound of police siren fades into sound of a bongo. A* **VOICE** *announces:)*

VOICE. The Chicago World's Fair proudly presents America's greatest living source of electrical power – Miss Sally Rand!"

(Drum roll. In a spotlight we see **SALLY RAND** *in all her naked glory: long curly hair, creamy skin, a radiant smile, luscious.* **SALLY** *softly swings her hips while fanning herself with two giant pinkish – white ostrich fans. Bongo drums accentuate her movements.* **DICK,** *watches mesmerized.)*

DICK. Holy Toledo! Great feathers!

(Slowly, **DICK** *is drawn to the stage, as* **SALLY** *undulates, singing to herself. She flirts with him, using her fans to attract him.* **DICK** *begins moaning.)*

E=mc squared…

SALLY. Oh, yeah. Whisper funny to me.

DICK. Energy equals mass plus the speed of light growing, growing….

SALLY. Keep it up, kid.

DICK. Linking…

SALLY. Jiggling…Say it again – gives me a charge: E equals …what?

DICK. E equals mc squared. Multiplying power.

SALLY. Oooo…energy, electricity, light…

DICK. Mass. That's, uh, men.

SALLY. Waves of light, that's me.

(She is about to hug him in her feathers when **MEL** *rushes in grabs* **DICK** *by the neck, starts dragging him out.* **SALLY** *continues to move sensuously, singing to herself.)*

E equals mc squared, E equals mc…

MEL. What the hell – We been huntin' all over for you. Your Mom thinks you got snatched like the Lindbergh baby. Franky's holdin' our place in line at the Hall of Science.

DICK. Pop, I'm seeing equations in color! I got a chance to get close to Miss Rand – !

MEL. You're a clean boy. Savin' your body for science!

DICK. I've got a chance to go deeper. Find out stuff first hand –

MEL. In the laboratory, buster! Wearin' a white lab coat. Can't wear a white coat if you aren't pure. Come on.

(**DICK** *breaks away.*)

DICK. Look! Never seen so many atoms so well put together…jigglin'…hot…I really understand now 'bout atoms lookin' for partners…to…rub against. For the first time.

MEL. That bombshell's a force of nature, all right. A wonder.

DICK. Nature's a woman? Wow. Why didn't you tell me?

MEL. We're disturbin' the danseuse.

DICK. Wait. I'm learning….a lot. Stuff ain't in books.

MEL. We got to get to the Hall of Science.

DICK. I don't want to leave.

MEL. When you first learned to ride a bicycle, you didn't want to get off. That's all I got to say on the matter.

DICK. Thanks for bringin' me to the Fair. Pop…? Sally… Sally…

(*But* **MEL** *has gone, leaving* **DICK** *standing alone. Should he leave or stay?* **SALLY** *comes to him, sing softly:*)

SALLY. E=mc squared.

(*She bumps his hip.*)

Boom.

DICK. Boom?

SALLY. Boom.

(He gets it. Bumps his hip against hers.)

DICK. Boom!

(She raises her fans in satisfaction. They move in unison. Bongo beat. Crossfade. A radio voice in the dark:)

VOICE. "The Green Hornet!" Brought to you by Lava Soap...

*(**DICK**, flashlight and book in hand, discovers **JOAN** in bed listening to the radio under the covers. It is 1935. **DICK** is seventeen now.)*

DICK. Hey, Joan. You asleep?

JOAN. Yeah.

DICK. Quick! Take off your radio! I wanna show you a big scientific thing before I go to college. We'll go out the window. I've already been out. I come back for you. I'll take the blame. I wanna talk to you anyway. In private. And I got an important present.

JOAN. Oh, boy!

(He leads her out.)

Where we going?

DICK. Shhhh. The beach.

(sound of waves, stars)

Look up.

(the vibrating Aurora Borealis)

JOAN. Holy Toledo! I'm dreaming, right?

DICK. It's called the Aurora Borealis.

JOAN. Looks like a waterfall of green headlights falling from the sky.

DICK. Or a girl's party skirt billowing my way...

JOAN. Oh...How wonderful!

DICK. Wonderful means full of wonder. Did you know that? Let's look at it.

(He takes her hand. They turn from us, take a few steps toward the water, look up. Silence.)

DICK. *(cont.)* I wonder why?

I wonder why?

I wonder why I wonder?

(beat)

JOAN. How does that happen?

DICK. I don't know yet.

JOAN. Promise you'll let *me* look it up. You can have the rest of the universe to study. But leave me the Borealis.

DICK. Okay. Start tomorrow. Brought you this college text-book on astronomy.

JOAN. It's too hard.

DICK. Start at the beginning. Read as far as you can, until you get lost. Then start at the beginning again. Keep working through until you understand the whole book.

JOAN. Why are you being so nice to me?

DICK. Did you forget already? I'm going away to college early. I won't see you for a long, long time.

JOAN. What's the big deal? So you're going to Columbia on the train tomorrow.

DICK. Columbia said "no."

JOAN. Weren't your grades good enough?

DICK. The Jewish quota was full up. So, I'm goin' to mit instead. Near Boston. Odd balls are welcome there, I guess.

JOAN. Crazy nuts.

(They laugh. Beat.)

I'll take care of Mommy and Poppy.

DICK. That's what I was goin' to ask you..

JOAN. I'm way ahead of you.

DICK. Joan, you're much smarter than me.

JOAN. I know. Just 'cause I'm a girl, it ain't fair I got to go to bed first. Before I came along there was another baby – a boy. Poppy doesn't like to talk about him.

DICK. Henry died before you were born. I miss my brother. But I'm goin' to get a bunch of new brothers up there. Fraternity brothers. I'm going to live with them in a Greek house. Frankly, I'm kinda scared about bein' in a world without women in it. What if I don't measure up? You know I can't toss a baseball straight.

JOAN. Yeah, but you're always doing stuff you're scared of doing. To prove you're not a sissy bookworm so big guys won't kick sand in your eyes. If I'd been born a boy, you wouldn't be leaving home looking for boys to play with. Guess everyone was disappointed when a girl showed up.

DICK. Look at page 407.

JOAN. It's got drawings –

DICK. In a scientific book, those are called diagrams.

JOAN. 407.

DICK. See, part of a spectrum of a star. Look at the bottom. What's the name of the astronomer put the data together?

JOAN. Cecilia Payne-Gaposhkin. Cecilia. A lady!

DICK. Yeah. So, you see, women do have the brains to be scientists. That's one law Poppy was wrong about.

(She throws her arms around him.)

JOAN. Oh, Ritty! This is the happiest moment of my life.

*(He turns away, suddenly moved. As **JOAN** runs out, she yells.)*

Promise me that someday we're going up in a rocket together. Like the one we saw at the Hall of Science at the Chicago World's Fair.

VOICES. Dr. Feynman! Dr. Feynman, the Challenger Commission's in session!

*(**DICK** turns from **JOAN**, becomes middle-aged, puts on his glasses. Lights begin to shift.)*

DICK. The young girl on the Shuttle, the teacher, Christa MacAuliffe, was too young to die.

*(He looks at **ARLENE GREENBAUM**, who stands in a pool of light.)*

DICK. *(cont.)* Arlene was too young to die.

*(**ARLENE** holds piano music to her breast. She wears hair clips made of feathers, frilly mittens and frilly bobby socks. As **JOAN** re-enters, **ARLENE** smiles at **DICK**, who disappears.)*

JOAN. *(sing-song)* Hello, Miss Greenbaum from Cederhurst.

*(She curtsies. We notice that **JOAN** is wearing identical mittens.)*

How are you feelin'? Holy Toledo, you look so pale. Wish I could look like you. Sick.

ARLENE. Have you been practicing, dear?

JOAN. My father left town and forgot to leave the two bits for my lesson. He thought you weren't goin' to make it today. Because you were lookin' so pale. He thinks girls who are dyin' are the cat's meow.

ARLENE. Don't worry about the money, honey. Besides you're going to make a lot of money when you play the piano for Miss Steinberg's ballroom class.

*(They sit on the piano bench. **JOAN** plays imaginary keys in a clunky style.)*

JOAN. I don't want to take the job away from you.

ARLENE. Oh, I'd rather participate as a dancer. Do it. That's better than accompanying the couples. I don't want to live a shadow life.

JOAN. I wanted to go with my Pop today, but he said he was going on a secret mission. To mit.

ARLENE. What's mit?

JOAN. A school for boys. My big brother is there. He can't seem to get out. That's why Poppy's goin' up there. To find out why they want to keep him for a couple more years.

ARLENE. You mean he's failing his subjects?

JOAN. He's got a bad stomach. And no girl friend. He's living with some Greek boys.He tried to get on the rowing team, but he fell in the river and almost drowned. Ritty can't get his arms and legs to follow his brain.

ARLENE. Is he in an institution?

JOAN. I know he's where special cases go. Odd balls. He's at an institute all right. For nut cases. He's always asking weird questions. Trying to figure out why things happen.

ARLENE. Me, too.

JOAN. Meantime, I'm the one's got to look after our parents. Keep 'em from being so afraid of everything: two-piece bathing suits, high blood pressure, the rise of fascism....

ARLENE. You poor thing.

JOAN. My big brother and I, we were lookin' up at the sky one night – before he was sent away – and we divided up the stars. He promised not to study my half of the night sky. That's why I love him.

ARLENE. What about *me*? I love to look up at the stars at night, don't I get to keep any for myself?

JOAN. Well....if you had a wedding with my big brother.... then all the stars would be in our family forever.

ARLENE. I'm already in love.

JOAN. Who with?

ARLENE. Frederic Chopin.

JOAN. Is he Jewish?

ARLNE: Kind of. Polish. Very passionate. Pale.

JOAN. Oh, I know who he is. He wrote this awful Mazurka here.

ARLENE. That's right.

JOAN. I feel not loyal playin' a song by a guy who's the competition. For you. I wanna keep you in the family. I love you a lot.

ARLENE. Chopin's body died. But his music lives. Sometimes.

JOAN. What he die of?

ARLENE. Consumption.

JOAN. Is that what you got?

ARLENE. The doctors don't know what I've got. Or their
not telling me.

(**JOAN** *embraces her.*)

Honey you're a terrible pianist. I can't steal your
father's money no more.

(**JOAN** *pulls out a small camera.*)

JOAN. Can I take a photograph of you? On the beach. In
your two-piece bathing suit?

ARLENE. Sure.

JOAN. My brother likes pin-ups.

(*M.I.T., Sigma Beta Delta fraternity house.* **DICK,** *in
underdrawers. on the bongos. Between beats, he jots
down notes on paper napkins, refers to an open book.
His roommate,* **JULIUS LOWENTHAL,** *also wearing
underdrawers, rushes in carrying a dark suit on a
hanger covered by dry cleaner's paper. he thinks he is a
big man on campus. he wears an M.I.T. varsity sweater.
Changes into his party clothes during the following.*)

JULIUS. Feynman! You haven't brushed my shoes! Stop that
banging! Feynman, we're expected at an important
tea-dance! Get cracking. All the new faculty fleeing
from Europe will be there. And Robert Oppenheimer
will be on hand to welcome them. And look us over.
These are hard times. No jobs. Sigma Beta Delta is the
best Jewish fraternity on campus. We've got to be twice
as correct as the next fellow. Had my second best suit
tailored for you. Put it on.

DICK. If I can't take my waitress friend, I ain't goin'.

JULIUS. You haven't told Dodo?!!

DICK. No. And she's comin' over soon.

JULIUS. That gum-chewing vamp's been trying to noodle an invitation to one of our formal functions for years. You're such a softy.

(DICK *jumps on his back, armlocks* JULIUS*'s throat.* JULIUS, *an athlete, lets* DICK *get away with this horseplay.*)

DICK. Lowenthal! Take that back! I ain't no softy.

JULIUS. I could have you expelled for choking a graduate student from the Brrronx.

DICK. Take it back, rich boy!

JULIUS. Bookworm!

DICK. The new librarian's beautiful.

JULIUS. Get my books?

DICK. On your bed.

JULIUS. Let go!

(*He unfastens* DICK *from his back.* DICK *starts to slip down to the floor.*)

DICK. I win. Say it.

JULIUS. You're weird. Ungrateful –

DICK. Weird I don't mind. Softy I mind.

JULIUS I take it back. We've got to go. Dick, walking in with a floozy on your arm is going to make you a target of derision.

(DICK *cuffs him affectionately.*)

DICK. Thanks for lettin' me roughhouse with you, Lowenthal.

JULIUS. We pledged to support each other: you'd help me with my studies and, in exchange, I'd teach you the social graces, how the highbrow world works. I want to return the favor tonight.

(*He knots a tie for* DICK, *places it over his head, adjusts it.*)

Tonight's crucial. We want to show you off. Your original scholarship adds luster to our house. But if you don't follow our rules, your entrée into the world of elite science will forever be closed to you. It's a very small world, Dick. Can't take one false step. Being talented isn't enough.

DICK. So, what's expected of me at this phoney-baloney teadance?

JULIUS. You must be as boring as possible. And you aren't going to get to first base if you show up escorting the campus whore.

DICK. Don't call her that! She gives me big helpings of french fries.

JULIUS. You're a ladies man. And you do the numbers. But you aren't a man's man. That's a big drawback.

DICK. I get my big breakthroughs between the sheets. Visualizations galore! I like dames, so what?

JULIUS. In America you have to be attractive to men, dummy. Men are your professors. They get you the scholarships. Put their names on your research, get your papers published. The whole system around here's mentors and proteges. And what do you do? Fall into the Charles River! Couldn't even make the rowing team. Big black eye for us.

(Almost unconsciously, **DICK** *slowly starts brushing* **LOWENTHAL**'s *party shoes.)*

DICK. The darkest hour of my childhood came when my father was in his Oldsmobile watching me play the outfield. I dropped a flyball. And the other side won. When I looked up my father had driven away. Julius, it gives me a warm glow that you guys picked me. I've always wanted to be part of a team. I'm grateful. So, here are your fuckin' dancin' shoes.

JULIUS.: Dick, tonight please don't put on that phoney-baloney Brooklyn accent you affect when you want to appear tough as nails.

DICK. I am tough as nails.

JULIUS. Bullshit! – Don't hit me. You're a piece of shit from a low-rent community and you show me no respect at all! At home, I'm special: the trophies I got! I'm expected to bring home a Nobel Prize some day! But here…..I have to work twice as hard as most, just to keep my head above water. I'm a plodder. While *You!* Professor Slater hands you his chalk and tells *you* to teach his class in atomic theory and you laugh –

DICK. Because I love atoms.

JULIUS. – And you say you see the numbers on the blackboard in colors! *I've* never seen numbers in colors.

(**DORIS** *enters, overdressed, wearing too much makeup, a hat, gloves, and a coat over her party dress.* **DORIS** *carries a grease – stained paper sack. She is played by the actress who played* **SALLY RAND**.)

DORIS. Hello, boys. Brought you some fries, Dicky.

DICK. I can't accept them.

DORIS. What's going on?

JULIUS. *(whispers)* Fix her radio after the dance.

(*He goes.*)

DICK. My tummy's startin' to turn over. Dodo, sweetheart, I can't take ya ta de dance.

DORIS. Why?!

DICK. My Pop's got a lot ridin' on my education. I didn't know I'd get in dutch datin' ya, Dodo. I didn't know the friggin' dance is restricted to the boring crowd. You're so gorgeous, you'd stand out like a sore thumb. I'd be a target for more name-calling. Sorry.

(*She picks up the book he was using, hurls it at him.*)

DORIS. Books! You think that's life? This is what I get for messing around with a boy ain't a man yet. Well, in *my* book a boy don't learn how to make a dame happy is dead from the head down

(*She starts to go.*)

DICK. Dodo – a kiss?

DORIS. I'd like to kick you in the heart – but my toes would break!

DICK. Ain't you worried about the rise a fascism?!!!

(**ROBERT OPPENHEIMER** *appears holding a tea cup and puffing on his characteristic pipe. A terrace. From inside, sounds of genteel conversation – snatches of German. Elegant violin tea-dance salon music.*)

OPPIE.: Yes. Let's go out on the terrace. I spent time in Germany. Do you speak German?

DICK. Man, I hardly speak English.

OPPIE. Well, not the King's English.

(*They laugh.*)

DICK. I didn't do too good in that subject.

OPPIE. Words so often betray us.

DICK. Numbers don't.

OPPIE. Numbers make me laugh. Have you read the latest paper on thermodynamics?

DICK. Yeah. It's a gas.

OPPIE. I chuckled all the way through it, laying on the deck of the Trimethy. I have a sloop. Trimethy is short for –

DICK. Trimethylamine.

OPPIE. Yes. A colorless liquid –

DICK. Smells like pickled herring.

(*They laugh.*)

OPPIE. I love being outdoors here on the terrace.

DICK. My mom's very big on breathing.

OPPIE. Mine, too.

DICK. *Her* breathing is the first thing I remember. Up close, you know. And here I am now looking out over the leaves, jiggling in the breeze and it busts my heart that the way I appreciate what I see wouldn't interest her.

OPPIE. What would you tell her, if you could?

DICK. Don't get me wrong, she's a very bright lady. Went to Ethical Culture on the West Side.

OPPIE. Me, too. Robert Oppenheimer.

DICK. Richard Feynman, Far Rockaway.

   (They shake.)

   Your pop's a big man in textiles.

OPPIE. And your mother's father is a big man in….?

DICK. Hats.

OPPIE. Ah, yes. You live in one of his houses. By the beach.

DICK. You've done your research.

OPPIE. That's what I do.

DICK. *My* pop's a self-taught scientist. Really gave me a leg-up living with him. What a brain. Those trees – even though he ain't up here – they belong to him. And he gave them to me.

OPPIE. How's that?

DICK. We used to go for walks, and he'd explain the world to me.

OPPIE. Would you give the trees to me, now? How would you explain what you see, in words anyone could understand? Even me. I'm overly educated so, alas, I lack a clarity of vision. While you, I'm told, intuit theoretical matters with great naturalness and share them with openhearted generosity – a natural born teacher, as your father must be. What would your father say to me about the glorious view?

DICK. He'd say:

   *(**MEL** appears.)*

MEL. Look at that tree there. Where did it come from?

OPPIE. It, uh, came out of the ground.

MEL. Guess what? It came out of the air.

OPPIE. What??

MEL. Yeah! The substance of a tree is carbon, carbon dioxide from the air. People look at trees and they think they come out of the ground, but really trees come out of the air.

OPPIE. How's that possible?

MEL. The carbon dioxide in the air goes into the tree, and changes it: it kicks out the oxygen, pushing the oxygen away from the carbon, and leaving the carbon substance with water.

OPPIE. Water comes out of the ground.

MEL. But how did it get there? It came out of the air, down from the sky. So in fact most of the tree is out of the air.

OPPIE. What about minerals?

DICK. There's just a little bit. You want me to keep going?

OPPIE. Who can stop you?

DICK. Great! Oxygen and carbon stick very, very tight. How is it that a tree is so smart as to manage to take the carbon dioxide, which is the carbon and oxygen so nicely combined, and undo it that easily?

OPPIE. Ah…!

DICK. "Ah," you say! "Life has some mysterious force…" But no – the sun shines, and it's the sunlight that comes down and knocks this oxygen away from the carbon, and now the oxygen is some terrible byproduct which the tree spits back into the air, leaving the carbon and water and stuff to make the substance of the tree!

OPPIE. Bravo, Mr. Feynman. Your father did a fine job training you.

DICK. Yeah. But…I'm not sure he's happy with me.

*(**MEL** disappears. Beat.)*

OPPIE. Have you ever seen the night sky in the New Mexican desert? I had a big crush on a beautiful Spanish woman ran a guesthouse in a place called Los Alamos. We used to go horseback riding at night. I'd like to go back there.

DICK. The night sky gives me a hard on.

OPPIE. It's tremendously thrilling.

DICK. Don't get me excited.

OPPIE. But space technology belongs to you.

DICK. Nope. It belongs to my baby sister. I made her a promise that in our house, *she* could have the upstairs for herself. I'll stick to the basement. Chemistry, biology, I get a kick out of all the physical sciences. I don't discriminate that way. Hell, I'm kinda democratic about learnin'. I just love it all. Gets my goat how the world wants to diminish us, tell us to just become one thing. Me, I'm an amateur for life.

OPPIE. A lover.

(beat)

That's what "amateur" means, in French.

DICK. Do you believe sex and science don't mix?

(OPPIE lights his pipe.)

OPPIE. Dr. Einstein believes that the upper half of our bodies plan and think, while the lower half determines our fate. Just be natural – about everything.

DICK. Not phony baloney.

OPPIE. You must be as funny as you can. Alive. Extreme change frightens people. And there's going to be a lot of that. So, laughter is a medicine that doesn't cost much. Who keeps the nation from being blue?

DICK. Groucho, Fred, and Jack.

(He suddenly turns away. Puts his face in his hands. OPPIE gives him a handkerchief.)

OPPIE. What is it? What I say?

DICK. Nothin'. It's just I'm so happy.

OPPIE. The kind of person I admire most is the man who becomes extraordinarily good at doing a lot of things, but still maintains a tear-stained countenance.

DICK. What about sex and science? You didn't really give me an honest answer.

OPPIE. I have twenty-twenty eyesight. I love women who are forty.

DICK. Stop! We're goin' to be kicked outta this mausoleum.

OPPIE. I've found sexual ecstasy clears my mind. You know, the great battle isn't between men and women, but between men and the men who like them. Nature is a woman. And we've dedicated our lives to studying her. She can't be fooled.

DICK. When I grow up, I wanna be like you.

OPPIE. I have something very important to propose to you. But you're not going to like it. That's why I was avoiding an honest answer to your crucial question.

DICK. Why aren't I goin' to like it?

OPPIE. America, Richard, is faced with the question of diverting our studies from the path of pure science to, perhaps, applying our theoretical might to new, murderous, methods of self-defense. Suddenly, there will appear new opportunities for our students. There will be war. So, young scientists will be called on to serve the nation. I think I can get you a full scholarship to graduate school. But you must swear not to marry until you graduate from Princeton.

DICK. Princeton??!

OPPIE. Eienstein is there, you know.

DICK. Princeton...Jeez.

OPPIE. There's a lot of foward-thinking activity there. Specially now with the need to develop new wartime technology. The greatest thinkers of our time are gathering there. In Physics, the great leaps of the imagination historically have been made by young men. In their twenties. But, my young friend, you must delay your experimentation with women.

DICK. I just broke a girl's heart. I'm a dope in that department.

OPPIE. You decide.

DICK. I'll lay off dames.

(Rapturous Chopin. **ARLENE,** *wearing her feather hair clips and frilly mittens, is playing the piano in the Feynman home, lost in the music.* **DICK** *enters, carrying a*

couple of long-stemmed roses and a small suitcase. He
watches surprised, fascinated as **ARLENE** *plays the final,*
quiet chords, tears rolling down her face. She takes out
a frilly hanky, passes it under her nose, closes the sheet
music, presses it to her heart.)

DICK. Your finger action. What does it do to your brain, I wonder? To move'em like that? We – men – do most of our work in our heads, kind of disconnected from the rest of us.

ARLENE. I wasn't working. The idea! Maybe that's the difference between men and women. We – women – don't separate our soul work from our home work.

DICK. A waitress friend comes over to me, says, "You still working on your meal?"

ARLENE. The idea! Eating is a pleasure. It's not working! The world is becoming so cut and dry. So scientific.

DICK. I love science!

ARLENE. Beauty's better!

(She smells one of the roses.)

Mmmmmmmm.

DICK. So pin a rose on your nose!

ARLENE. You're blushing. You're trembling.

DICK. I feel like friggin' Goldilocks. I come home and, surprise –

ARLENE. An intruder's sleeping in your bed.

DICK. I don't know much about music, but I find a dish pressing down the keys of my sister's piano – that's plenty personal in my book.

ARLENE. We had to sell our piano. Your mother let's me play yours when she takes your father to Dr. Gold. She's going to love these long-stemmed roses.

DICK. I swiped 'em from Einstein's garden. You keep 'em.

ARLENE. Oh, I couldn't.

DICK. To make up for me flyin' off the handle at you. Get's my goat, you thinkin' scientists are cut and dry.

ARLENE. Tell you what. I'll take them home and paint a picture of them for your mother.

DICK. You play the piano and you paint…

ARLENE. I'm sorry I invaded your privacy.

DICK. You already done that.

(*pulls out photo*)

Joan sent me this pin-up of you on the beach. She said all the boys were crazy about you. And the parents, too. Because you're so talented and clean. "A girl of perfect repute." Your bare middle's really something.

ARLENE. A wartime measure. Two-piece bathing suits save on fabric.

DICK. I'm happy to meet you, Miss Flesh. I mean, in the flesh.

(*They shake.*)

Dick Feynman. Far Rockaway.

ARLENE. Arlene Greenbaum. Cederhurst.

DICK. What you lookin' at?

ARLENE. Signs. Joan led me to believe you're…Sweet.

DICK. I'm plenty dumb. A klutz. She tell you that?

ARLENE. Well…

DICK. I know. I don't know what to do with myself. What else did Joan say about me?

ARLENE. That you're seriously deranged.

DICK. That's 'cause I don't have a dame to arrange me.

ARLENE. So what about your waitress friend?

DICK. You know what I learned in college?

ARLENE. What?

DICK. That boring is good. Being quiet. Unemotional. I didn't believe it until now. You're so boring.

ARLENE. Thank you.

DICK. You sooth my troubled waters, Arlene Greenbaum from Cederhurst. At this point, when I face the family, I get the runs. Can't sit still at the dinner table five minutes. Do me a favor.

ARLENE. What?

DICK. Take off your gloves.

ARLENE. Don't get personal.

DICK. Sorry.

ARLENE. Your sister wants us to get married.

DICK. I want to.

ARLENE. Dick, I think I'm dying. You might as well know it.

DICK. When?

ARLENE. Doctors are so dumb.

DICK. What you got? Whatever you got makes you more beautiful.

ARLENE. Fever…and fear…Heighten a girl's coloring.

DICK. Give me all the symptoms, I'll look 'em up. I want to take care of you, Arlene from Cederhurst.

ARLENE. The doctors say that if I have…physical relations with a man I'll die quicker. A baby's out of the question for me. My hands perspire. That's why I wear mittens. *That's* a symptom.

DICK. I'm ga ga about you.

ARLENE. Why?

DICK. What a problem you are! You make me feel stupid. I wanna solve you. I love solvin' difficult problems. And on top of that Princeton made me promise to give the school my body and soul. Swear I wouldn't get married or else.

ARLENE. Or else what?

DICK. I'll lose my scholarship.

ARLENE. So we'll postpone making plans.

DICK. Time's the one thing we ain't got. That's why I'm rushing things.

ARLENE. Without a scholarship *you're* dead.

DICK. You don't understand. *You* give me life. For the first time, BAM – CRASH – VOOM! I got a chain reaction goin' that's fusin' my body and my brain into one person. I'm racin' toward home plate. See, until now I been perplexed – sad – that life's laws tell us we got to chop up our guts into lonely little pieces – the student part, the funny part, the job part, the serious part, the son part, the patriotic part, the male part, the female part. Oh, hell, I'll go along with you. Stop trying to figure out stuff in a cut and dry scientific way. Beauty's great. I don't want to break stuff into particles with my head, I want to let go. Gosh, it's taken me so long to integrate the whole ball of wax and Boom, suddenly, I'm splitting open like an atom. New energy is coming! This is love, isn't it?

(She nods.)

That's a "Yes"?

ARLENE. I can't speak. Sorry.

DICK. Oh, boy!

(He puts his arms around her, tries to kiss her.)

ARLENE. Not on the lips.

(He kisses her fingertips.)

You're so delicate.

DICK. Don't tell nobody.

(She wipes his forehead with her frilly handkerchief.)

ARLENE. Now *you're* perspiring. Maybe you already caught something from me.

DICK. You know what? We're startin' to work on a secret wartime weapon that could wipe out Hitler and humanity, too. We could all be dead, not just you. So, the best thing to do is to love the hell outta each other while we can.

ARLENE. Promise you won't forget me at Princeton.

(Princeton. Oppenheimer's office.)

OPPIE. *(to imaginary secretary)* Get young Feynman in here in a hurry!

*(***DICK** rushes in carrying a dinner plate and puffing on a pipe like* **OPPIE** *'s.)*

DICK. I'm here, Boss. I was makin' an appointment with your secretary. Got to show you –

OPPIE. Feynman, you piss me off.

DICK. I ain't never heard you say "piss" before.

OPPIE. "Ain't never" is a double negative, and you know it! Piss. Shit. Fuck.

(DICK *laughs.*)

I don't have time for this. Ain't funny, McGee.

DICK. "Ain't"! Well. there's still hope for you.

OPPIE. But is there hope for *you?*

DICK. To do what?

OPPIE. Close the door. Lock it. I hate punishing people.

DICK. Piece of shit lock.

OPPIE. And keep your voice down. And, I've told you a dozen times, that when you are in the dining hall, cover your mouth when you are discussing…our war work. The campus is crawling with spies who can read lips. I received reports that –

(DICK *laughs.*)

I've got a juvenile delinquent on my hands.

DICK. You and your gang, like little kids up in a tree house, "What's de passwoid?"

OPPIE. Well, you're not going to have to endure the gang much longer. I am firing you from the project. You were never man enough, disciplined enough, to adhere to the rigors of applied war-time physics. Please go to your desk this minute. Empty it. Bring me every scrap of paper. You may remain until you finish your doctoral work.

(DICK *takes the pipe out of his mouth, lays it on* OPPIE*'s desk.*)

DICK. Sorry I didn't measure up. It's been a problem all my life, living up to people's expectations.

OPPIE. Professor Einstein claims you broke into his safe. The safe contains – well, you know what it contains.

DICK. I didn't read any of it.

OPPIE. So you admit you breached our security. Broke in – !

DICK. *(nervous laugh)* Don't try and keep me out.

OPPIE. You have no respect for privacy. Decency cannot be taught. Breeding. Brilliance doesn't excuse boorish behavior.

DICK. Oh, brother, those new filing cabinets you bought – with the steel rod going down and the combination locks –

OPPIE. You broke into the new cabinets?!!

DICK. They were an immediate challenge, naturally. I love puzzles.

(OPPIE tries to light his own pipe. Can't.)

I'll become boring, Rabbi. I promise.

(DICK lights a match for him.)

OPPIE. Get out of my sight! Washington is in an uproar. What other secured place did you break into?

DICK. The cyclotron in the basement.

OPPIE. Under pain of firing squad, you are forbidden to set foot down there again.

DICK. Want me to tell you how I figure out all the combinations?

OPPIE. No. Are you stealing the plates now from the dining hall? That's very handsome dinnerware. Probably nothing this luxurious will ever be made again in our lifetime. I know you don't appreciate such things, but you see this gold around the rim. And this hand-painted insignia –

DICK. Yeah. It's because of the fancy insignia that I noticed.

OPPIE. Noticed what?

DICK. Two jocks were tossing this plate in the dining hall. When it spun through the air, it wobbled. Oppie, because of the insignia, I could see the spin and the wobble weren't in synch. Do you think the two rotations are related? I tried to work out the problem on paper.

(Takes out a bunch of paper napkins, unfolds them in front of OPPIE.)

OPPIE. Paper napkins!

(Despite himself, he is drawn to the napkins.)

DICK. Got into the habit of eating and – Read the equations in the middle.

OPPIE. Mmmmm. Very complicated. Looks like children's drawings.

DICK. My visual sort of shorthand. But I did the numbers. See.The problem's hard to crack.

OPPIE. But you came up with a two-to-one ratio in the relationship between the wobble and the spin.

DICK. Too neat. I want to understand these forces directly.

OPPIE. What's the value of spending time on this?

DICK. *(laughter)* Keeps me out of trouble.

OPPIE. Silence.

DICK. In the night.

OPPIE. Hush. Or I'll smack you.

DICK. Say, I reported to the security staff that the documentation wasn't safe. Explained every break in. I can penetrate any –

*(**OPPIE** opens thermos. Hands shaking, serves himself a cup. **DICK**, as he has done many times, reaches for a mug with his name on it.)*

Aren't you gonna serve me some of your great black market coffee?

OPPIE. Shut up. I'm thinking!

DICK. "Shut up"!!! Boy, things must really be bad.

*(**OPPIE** grabs napkins. Turns them around, trying to understand the meaning of the numbers.)*

OPPIE. They are.

DICK. Your hands are shaking.

OPPIE. Quiet….

DICK. It's like an earthquake to see my unshakeable Boss Rabbi jigglin' to beat the band. Stop it, will you. Scares me. Always counted on your politeness, can't even offer a poor student a mug of java. What's happenin'? It's the end of civilization as we know it.

*(**DICK** drums on the desk. Speaking absently, **OPPIE** continues studying the napkins.)*

OPPIE. Stop beating on your drum in your dorm. Washington frowns on jazz.

DICK. What else is a healthy guy supposed to do in the middle of the night? What's wrong with it?

OPPIE. It's colored music.

DICK. So?

OPPIE. Anarchic, un-American. Improvisation makes people uneasy. Passion.

DICK. Have you noticed how women got a coffee smell? Specially black coffee.That's why people drink it. To drink a dame's darkness.

OPPIE. Well, you're not getting any.

DICK. Why?

OPPIE. You're punished.

DICK. Why? I blow the lid off the crappy security –

OPPIE. Because you're dirty-minded.

DICK. A dirty mind is a sign of intelligence.

OPPIE. The principles you're going to teach. But it's true.

DICK. I'm gonna be a teacher-and-a-half. The Pop of the new physics.

OPPIE. If you don't land in jail.

(refers to napkins)

See here, young fellow. I think you can make a connection between the axial wobble of a cafeteria plate and the abstract quantum-mechanical notion of spin in the electron.

DICK. Brother! That was a leap! You just jumped!

OPPIE. *You* make me jump. I'm keeping these napkins.

DICK. When's the gang movin' out?

OPPIE. You opened *my* safe, too!!

DICK. Because of the high esteem in which I hold you, I read the contents. So, seems like you're goin' to get your wish. To head on out to that place where the Spanish dame lived – Los Alamos, New Mexico. She waitin' for you on her palomino?

OPPIE. You horny kid! You always have lust on your brain, don't you?! What do you know about the higher reaches of sublime love?

*(**DICK** stands, hurt.)*

DICK. Send me a postcard from the desert. You're the perfect guy to devise the most hurtful instruments ever invented. You said once the best way to live was to be natural – about everything. Well, ain't you noticed that everything we do around here goes counter to nature? Not coming with you is kind of like interrupting sex at the big moment. Ain't natural. In my mind, nature is a fabulous naked lady just wearin' feathers. That's why we like studying her up and down. She ain't too happy with us these days. Thanks for the punishment. You're a born killer.

OPPIE. Wait.

DICK. What for?

OPPIE. Tell me about your woman. Arlene.

DICK. She's not my woman. Mine. Yet. Not that it's any of your business.

OPPIE. I'm surprised.

*(A vision of **ARLENE** appears to **DICK**. In a two-piece bathing suit, Army cap. she sits on the railing of a pier, hair blowing in the wind, a true l940s pin-up girl. she waves at **DICK**.)*

DICK. She's dying of lymphomic tuberculousis. Her father told her she's just got inflamed lymph glands. He made me promise not to tell her the truth.

(**DICK** *looks at her with longing, then raises his hand, waves. She waves back, smiling. The Feynman house. Dinner time. Simultaneously, we now see the three scenes at the same time.* **JOAN** *waves at* **ARLENE**.)

JOAN. Arlene says she's got bac-ter-eea in her mouth, so she doesn't let my brother, the scientist, stick his tongue in there.

LUCILLE. Drink your milk, dear.

MEL. If they don't kiss, what do they do?

JOAN. Because Ritty's mail is all being censored now, Arlene thought it would be fun if we all learned Chinese. To drive the censors crazy. Ritty's defense work is becoming more secret. It could drag on for months. So they're practicing a private code. For the hard times ahead.

MEL. They're making plans...

LUCILLE. Mel, he could get killer germs from her. Die.

JOAN. Mama, you see germs in the milk of human kindness.

LUCILLE. Joan...that's pretty good.

MEL. Joan, I know you think we're over-protective about things that could hurt you children. But, we have good reason to be afraid. And I'm going to tell you why life has taught us to be apprehensive. You're older now and we're going to need your help soon. My father's heart tells me there are some difficult trials ahead for us as a family. You had an older brother who died.

JOAN. Henry.

MEL. Some day when you have children you'll know... how...

LUCILLE. Mel, Dr. Gold said not to –

MEL. Nothing is worse than the death of a child. We don't know what killed Henry. Meningitis, most likely. Modern science failed. We were so helpless to save him. But, now – We're going to wage a life and death war in this house.

LUCILLE. We couldn't survive another death.

DICK. The doctors think that if Arlene has physical relations, she'll die quicker. So, I'm in kind of a hurry. I can't marry her – hold her in my arms tight – husband and wife healing – because of the god-damned, unnatural rules of this creepy institution that won't allow wives in our dorms! Horny? You bet I'm horny –

OPPIE. *(a realization)* So, you can't penetrate her, so you penetrate us. Poetic.

DICK. You're losin' me.

OPPIE. I don't want to lose you. Now that I understand why you've become a safecracker, I feel more confident about making you a proposition: I want you on my team in New Mexico. To train unschooled defense workers, among other duties. Immediately. We must accelerate our development of nuclear weapons. All our efforts must now be focussed on winning the war. That means delaying your doctorate. But, Dick, it means you can marry. You'd be leaving Princeton, so your scholarship becomes immaterial. If you agree to go, you'll be on the government's payroll. I recall there's a sanatorium in Albuquerque. You could visit Arlene on weekends.

DICK. I don't know if Putzie can stand the long train ride.

OPPIE. I'll arrange for you to occupy a private compartment. My wedding gift. With a bed big enough so you can hold her in your arms all the way. Go home and arrange your affairs.

MEL. Why did he come home...in the middle of the term? Joan, you know.

JOAN. I love her.

LUCILLE. *(gasps, a realization)* He's come home to –

MEL. Don't say it! Don't think it!

DICK. *(off)* I'm home!

MEL. Ritty, get in here.

LUCILLE. Your blood pressure.

MEL. Let me do the talkin'

LUCILLE. *I* know how to talk to my son.

MEL. You don't know the difference between an electron and a photon. *I* taught him to think for himself.

JOAN. And now that he's thinking for himself, you don't like it. I don't get it.

MEL. He's not thinking. For the first time. That's the problem.

LUCILLE. He's going to have a wonderful life. Just not yet.

JOAN. When? If not now, when?

MEL. JOAN!

JOAN. Didn't a wise Jewish man say that, "If not now –

LUCILLE. JOAN!

JOAN. I'm not in the room.

MEL. I feel like an old fashioned father for once.

LUCILLE. Good.

MEL. How old is the boy? Twenty-two? Twenty-three?

(**DICK** *enters, happy, smiling.*)

DICK. Pop I stopped by the bank like you asked. What's for dinner?

MEL. Who can eat? Sit.

LUCILLE. Obey your father.

MEL. For starters, so you've become educated. There's one question I've always had that I've never understood very well and, since I may never have another chance, I want you to explain it to me.

DICK. What?

MEL. When an atom makes a transition from one state to another it emits a particle of light called a photon.

DICK. Right.

MEL. Is the photon in the atom ahead of time or is there no photon in it to start with?

DICK. There's no photon in there, it's just that when the electron makes a transition it comes.

MEL. Where does it come from then, how does it come out?

DICK. I have a happy day with the woman I love and I come home and you're waitin' for me with your daggers drawn. Look, Putzie made some pencils for me. They say "Putzie loves Coach" here in gold letters. She calls me Coach, can you beat it?

LUCILLE. Nobody touch. Killer germs. Go wash your hands.

DICK. *(in Chinese, to* **JOAN***)* What's going on?

JOAN. *(in Chinese)* War.

MEL. I want a report. In English!

DICK & JOAN. Censorship!

MEL. Why were you given a leave of absence? In the middle of the term?

DICK. I can tell you about my Ph.D. research, that's all.

MEL. This is Feynman University. And today you're taking your final oral examination. We're going to determine if the school is going to put it's name on you, or strip you of it...

DICK. I got the Feynman name on me.

MEL. If you fail, you're going to be out of this family for ever!

DICK. Ain't fair. Didn't give a guy time to prepare...

MEL. You been preparing all your life for tonight. You were prepared fine until you got distracted and started takin' the wrong path.

JOAN. *(whispers)* I never thought of us Feynmans as a school...

LUCILLE. What do you think this kitchen is? A classroom.

JOAN. Oh...yeah. Ritty was my first teacher...

DICK. And Poppy was mine.

LUCILLE. Didn't *I* teach anybody anything?

(beat)

Well?

DICK. The soft stuff: compassion, mercy...

JOAN. Milk.

DICK. Humor.

MEL. *(to* **LUCILLE***)* You taught him to have a big mouth!

JOAN. *(whispers)* I told you, they don't kiss! Is that why you're getting an oral examination? To see if you got germs in there?

DICK. Joan, an oral examination isn't about kissing. Before a guy is granted a Ph.D. he has to research and write his doctoral thesis. Then he's got to go into a room no bigger than this and stand before dried up, sexless old foeggies...

JOAN. ...like Mommy and Poppy....

DICK. ...Right...And God help you, if your answers contradict their view of the world. But the research part is fun.

JOAN. What's fun about it?

DICK. Well, in part, I want to come up with a mathematical theory that explains how the world works. A unifying key that will unlock the unknown. A new law.

LUCILLE. He's a Moses.

MEL. No one's been able to solve, uh, what you want to solve. Not even Einstein!

DICK. The problem's too big for you to understand.

LUCILLE. Ritty!

MEL. So explain it to me.

DICK. It'd be like Chinese to you. You don't have the numbers.

MEL. Try me.

DICK. I can't try to explain the answer to your question about photons. You don't have the knowledge, the vocabulary, the numbers to get it. And I ain't got it in me yet to know how to explain it to you in simple terms. Families are like a bath. At first they're great, then they're not so hot. Phooey! Phooey! A thousand times Phooey!

LUCILLE. Ritty, you look ugly. Give me your pocket comb.

DICK. Pocket comb?! My pockets don't need combing. Pop, here's the deposit slip.

MEL. I ask you to do banking transactions for me so you'll learn the value of money.

DICK. You taught me the value of numbers. And for that I am grateful. But money? Don't you feel humiliated living in my grandfather's house? I do. We were so poor during the worst of the depression you couldn't afford my going through puberty.

LUCILLE. Spell Mississippi for me.

DICK. The state or the river?

LUCILLE. He's out of control.

JOAN. We're not poor. That's a lie. What's puberty?

DICK. I don't know. I never had it. In this house, it's having to grow up too fast. I was a good student. Did everything I was told. Then, I get shipped out of town to duke it out with animals older than me, bigger than me. Because "A lot was riding on my education." Phooey! I'm tired of being good. I'm tired of disappointing people. Because no matter how good I do, how hard I work – how can I live up to people's expectations? It's really hard to understand the laws of life around here. I know I trip up. I get confused by the mixed signals you put out: "Sex and science don't mix." What is that!? And not just Feynman University. The big universities in my life condemn bodies getting together. It ain't scientific! It ain't human! It's far easier to find an equation that couples space and light, than to find a formula that integrates work and love. Life ain't so cut and dry. It's weird. And wonderful. And I'm going around spraining a gut trying to put it all together. The truth is, I ain't so bright. I just spend more time than most guys concentrating on difficult stuff. Sometimes I think I'd accomplish more being irresponsible. Oh, the hell with it.

MEL. I think he's going through pubertry TODAY. Hey, Ritty, how's the pretty sick girl?

DICK. Her parents don't take care of her enough.

LUCILLE. She's a lovely girl. So accomplished.

DICK. I'm going to tie the knot with her.

MEL. What?!!!

DICK. I'm going to marry Arlene tomorrow. I've got a judge lined up. I've got to get back to work. Wanna come? It's war time. Everything's happening in a hurry.

MEL. Who's ever heard of a married student?

LUCILLE. Your blood pressure.

MEL. Lucille, it isn't just that his school life would go down the drain, Ritty could catch something from her. A killer disease.

LUCILLE. He can't marry her. He could die.

(*DICK starts picking food from* **MEL***'s plate.*)

DICK. Fruit and rice. That's it?

LUCILLE. Your father's diet.

(**MEL** *stares at the salt shaker. Covers one eye with a hand, then does the same with his other hand.*)

DICK. What is it?

MEL. I've got a blind spot. Means a small blood vessel just burst in my brain.

DICK. I'm callin' Dr. Gold!

MEL. Wait up! I got something I been savin' for you. Better give it to you now. Here, catch.

(*Tosses him a wrapped package.* **DICK** *catchs it, then starts to untie carefully the many blue ribbons that wrap the package.*)

He caught it! Hey for the first time butterfingers caught a fly!

DICK. What is this? Why'd you put so many ribbons on this? Phooey! I got to keep movin', got a lot of stuff on my mind, and no time left to do it. Anybody telephone me?

MEL. Son, Arlene is goin' to die.

DICK. We're all going to die. Some day. So why worry about it? Death don't frighten me one bit. The important thing is to live now. We'll have a fun time for a couple years. I want to make *her* happy. The world ain't going to exist too much longer anyhow.

(He pulls out a gleaming white lab coat.)

Pop...! Holy Toledo!

MEL. Put it on. Dr. Feynman.

DICK. I ain't a PhD yet.

MEL. I know. But I may not make it to your graduation ceremonies.

DICK. The war's thrown a wrench smack into the research I been doin' for my doctorate. My professors want me to interrupt the pure research I been doin'-my Space-Time Approach to Quantum Electrodynamics – and join a team of scientific alter cacas. Go to a secret place in New Mexico to work on defense problems. The gang's leavin' Princeton and headin' out into the desert. Everybody's in a hurry.

MEL. You think Hitler's going to win?

DICK. I'm goin' to give 'im the finger.

MEL. Oh, yeah? How's that, tough guy?

DICK. Can't talk.

MEL. I'm a German spy? I've never done anything in my life worth keepin' secret. Ritty, if not sharin' secrets makes you feel like you got a private key to the Holy a Holies, talk your mumbo jumbo to Oppie. Don't talk to me. Oh, yeah, there's one big secret you don't know. I went up to M.I.T. to have a glass tea with Professor Oppenheimer to discuss your future. He wanted my approval about you going on with your studies. He said the life of a scientist was so tough, he needed to know if the family would support you, heal you at home when times were rough. The guy is such a class act, clearly living a dream life. My dream life. I wanted that dream life for you. So, I said yes. And I lost my son. You have surpassed me in knowledge.

DICK. Let me clue you in to a big secret man-to-man, 'cause
I want you to know a little bit about my place in the
world as a man. I'll keep it clean. I once received the
favors of a nice fun dame used to give me french fries
to help me through some lonely patches when I wasn't
home. Well, I was faced with losing face at my fraternity
if I took her to a fancy faculty function. So, I didn't.
I had to tell her I couldn't take her, even though I
promised I would. I did it for your sake, because so
much has been riding on my education, I didn't want
to spoil my chances – make a bad impression. Well,
I haven't gotten over it, what I did to that girl. And I
swore to myself I wouldn't do what the world wants,
ever again. Of course, there's no comparison – my
feelings for Arlene and my feelings for Dodo. But Pop,
you didn't want to bring up a non-learner. Butterfingers has been learning a thing or two about stuff ain't
in books. Deep stuff.

MEL. I always wanted to make life an adventure for you.

DICK. What's it goin' to take for you to be happy with me?

MEL. BE RESPONSIBLE FOR A CHANGE! GIVE UP THE
GIRL!

DICK. Thanks for the white coat. It's going to make a beautiful dress for my bride.

MEL. Honor it.

(The lab coat on his arm, **DICK** *and* **ARLENE** *on the
beach, silver moonlight on the waves.)*

ARLENE. How sublime.

*(A sea breeze. She shivers. He puts the lab coat over her
shoulders.)*

No. This white lab coat is yours.

DICK. It's your weddin' dress. Marry me tomorrow. I promise not to touch you. Military secret: We're workin' on
an explosive device. That'll put a stop to wars for all
time. I'm tellin' you so you'll realize that I got a lot
on my mind. Makes all my blood rush to my head all

the time. Ain't got body fluids left over – to come to a boilin' point. I'm hot to hold you. You'll marry me, won't ya?

ARLENE. I don't want to die a virgin.

(**LUCILLE** *appears.* **DICK** *starts putting on a tie, brushing his shoes, combing his hair. Unconsciously,* **LUCILLE** *helps her son to pack a small suitcase.*)

LUCILLE. That nice Lowenthal boy from the Bronx telephoned. Julius. He said he's sorry, but he can't attended your wedding. Too last minute. Julius said he had to host a big meeting. Apparently, he's become a captain in the defense industry and he can get you a big-time job. So, you don't have to run off. He wants to take you to lunch on Monday.

DICK. Get dressed, Mama. I want you should look beautiful.

LUCILLE. How can I go to a wedding that's going to kill your father? Ritty, I forbid you to go out that door!

(*She kneels.*)

I'm begging you.

DICK. Mama, you're tearing your last good stockings…

LUCILLE. Well, I'm not getting up until you become my son again.

(**DICK** *kneels.*)

DICK. You look so beautiful up close.

LUCILLE. I'm trying to save your life, Ritty.

DICK. Mama, I'm a success.

LUCILLE. Not as a son.

DICK. Isn't it great that we love each other so much that it's natural for us to kneel down on the floor together. And nobody's laughing. Here's my pocket comb. Want to comb my hair?

(*She starts to comb his hair.*)

I'll write you letters.

(She gets up.)

LUCILLE. Liar. You never gave the postman much work. No. Don't write. Why fake your affection? We're not the Feynman family from Far Rockaway any more! Why aren't you packing any winter clothes?

DICK. After we get married, we're takin' the train to New Mexico. So it'll be a double thing, a honeymoon and a chance to play on the team working on the most important science project known to man!

LUCILLE. I HATE SCIENCE!

DICK. Mama, that's crazy.

LUCILLE. Crazy? You've become frightening, unnatural in my sight. First, you propose to a seriously sick girl who could carry you off with her to the grave –

DICK. We're holdin' back till she's better.

LUCILLE. Then, you interrupt your studies to engage in making frightening weaponry. Better you should be a foot soldier fighting fascism, than a boy on a production line manufacturing machines so monstrous that you've got to go hide your face in the mountains somewhere to do it! There's something very ungodly about the whole thing! Why don't you see that? Why aren't you afraid? A success? You're so pathetic. We're living the end of our lives and you don't even know it! She's going to break your heart.

(She goes. Sound of a train.)

(ARLENE *appears in a hospital bed in Albuquerque, New Mexico, combing her hair. A screen at the foot of her bed. A knock on the door.)*

ARLENE. Come in.

*(**DICK** stays on the opposite side of the screen.)*

DICK. Oh… – Your perfume – the unsettling power of your body – in a bed – so close –

ARLENE. Stop. Calm down. Breathe.

DICK. Okay. It drives the censors crazy that we write to each other in Chinese pictograms. Because you draw and paint, it's really helping me to make visual diagrams of dry mathematical concepts, so I can explain tough ideas to my pals. I do my work, but my superiors are disconcerted about me

ARLENE. Why?

DICK. Because I am essentially a free man, that makes me a very suspicious character around that sweaty, male enclave. The site was formerly a boys' school, did you know that? The whole place is like a hot locker room. I always wanted to belong to, be accepted by, energetic, virile pals, striving toward a common goal. Well, I can't wait to get out of there. Come to you.

ARLENE. I live for our visits.

DICK. Me, too.

ARLENE. Are you calmed down enough to remove the screen now?

(He removes the screen.)

Dick, don't kiss me yet. I've got a little fever.

DICK. Doesn't your temperature shoot up when I come on weekends?

ARLENE. Yeah.

DICK. That's a good sign. That I kill you.

(They laugh.)

ARLENE. Where do you spend the night in Albuquerque? What is it? You're turning red.

DICK. You give me sunstroke, lady.

ARLENE. Have a seat. Aren't you exhausted from travelling like a pioneer across a hundred miles of desert?

DICK. Remind me to give you something I brought you.

ARLENE. Ooo where is it?

DICK. In my pocket. Don't fall off the bed. Hands off. There's a story that goes with it first. Ain't expensive, so, see, the story adds value to it.

ARLENE. Please don't spend on stuff. I'm getting worried about money.

DICK. Why? I'm making three hundred dollars a month. Wow!

ARLENE. But we spend twice that. This sanatorium is so expensive. And my savings are running out. Of course, if I die, then I won't be a financial drain. How much do you spend to sleepover?

DICK. Fifty cents. It's cheap.

ARLENE. A boarding house?

DICK. No, a whorehouse. Fifty cents and clean sheets.

ARLENE. Coach!

DICK. Because of the war, the town's full up. Don't worry about it. By day I have my Putzie Madonna.

ARLENE. And by night?

DICK. CLEAN SHEETS! I learned early that you can always find a bed in a brothel. How am I going to make money for us? My pop made about $5,000 a year. I don't need more than that.

ARLENE. Don't you think you'll get a top teaching job?

DICK. My pop asked me a question about physics I couldn't explain to him. I've really felt bad about that ever since. He used to explain stuff to *me*, summers. The other kids would want to go walking in the woods with us. But my pop wouldn't want to take them along. He had a personal father-son thing with me. So he poured all his wonder of nature into me. I feel I want to convey my wonder about the world to others, students maybe.

ARLENE. Since you don't have a son of your own. So, tell me my story for today.

DICK. Once upon a time....

ARLENE. I love this. Once upon a time....

DICK. This is a true story.

ARLENE. So?

DICK. I met an old guy in the desert. I take a short cut. He's got a well, so I stop, fill my canteen. Leave him some pennies. He finally got the courage to come down from his cave and talk with me. A real gentleman of the old school. Bowed and introduced himself as Don Moises de Toledo.

ARLENE. He was afraid of you?

DICK. He thought I worked for the Spanish Inquisition.

ARLENE. Maybe he's been hiding here a couple of hundred years.

DICK. Maybe people don't die around here.

ARLENE. What did he tell you?

DICK. Must have had a lot of money at one time. He said he landed in the port of Vera Cruz. Seems a lot of Jews came over at the time of the Inquisition and he joined a caravan of conquistadores and got farther north than anybody. Coming to New Mexico, those cavaliers travelled in great style. Every night, he said, they'd light a big fire, eat and drink. Musicians would play and actors would perform a play for their enjoyment every night. That's why I'm a little late today because he wanted pass on his story to me.

ARLENE. When an old person wants to have a word with you, it's important to stop running and listen. How did you gain his confidence?

DICK. I told him I was a Jew, too. Putzie, the poor old guy cried for joy. He's from Toledo and he kept the key to his house, so when the persecution blew over, he could go back, unlock his door. When I said good-bye he gave me the key to his house in Toledo, Spain. Said he finally faced the fact he's not going to make it back. Wanted me to have it. It's for you.

(hands her a rusty, historic-looking key)

ARLENE. Thanks. Did you find it on the road?

DICK. Keep it.

ARLENE. The head nurse told me my father is coming to visit. All along, my father has said I've got sick glands. Curable.

DICK. Your father made me promise to go along with that diagnosis. Otherwise, he wouldn't have let you marry me.

ARLENE. What have I got? I've been using all this free time to look up my symptoms in medical books. Tell me, Coach. What have I got?

DICK. Lymphatic tuberculosis.

ARLENE. No cure for it.

DICK. Don't you think we've been having a good time?

ARLENE. I suspect my father's coming all the way out here to say good-bye. The doctors must have told him I'm getting worse.

(He pulls out a letter.)

DICK. Joan sure knows me. She knows I wouldn't read her letters unless she wrote them in really tough code. Help me figure it out.

ARLENE. Do you mind if we decode the letter later?

DICK. Putzie, this is *your* time. What do you want to do?

ARLENE. Have a baby.

DICK. Holy Toledo.

ARLENE. How are you feeling? Coach, are you too tired?

DICK. To make a baby? No.

ARLENE. I think we should. Before it's too late.

DICK. Okay. Let's try.

(He sits on the bed. Starts untying his shoes.)

ARLENE. The nurses are nuts about you. I'm jealous. Oh –

DICK. What?

ARLENE. You got one of your father's clean handkerchiefs?

(He pulls out a clean handkerchief. She unfolds it.)

Put this over your mouth and nose.

DICK. Am I so ugly?

ARLENE. Coach, what I've got could kill you.

DICK. Good thing my Mom taught me never to leave the house without a clean handkerchief.

(He covers **ARLENE**'s *mouth and nose with the large handkerchief. Kisses her passionately through the handkerchief.)*

Oh, boy...! Marriage. The great equation!

(Their ardor grows. He rips off the handkerchief.)

(As their loving mounts, **SALLY RAND** *appears behind the bed, rises her large white ostrich fans, brings them down on the lovers, caressing them with her feathers from foot to head. Then, stands tall, lifting up the fans, forming the shape of an atomic bomb explosion. Beating bongos top a reverberating boom as...)*

(THE CURTAIN FALLS.)

ACT II

*(1985. **DICK**, in middle age, is teaching in a lecture hall jammed with Caltech students, California. He wears horned-rimmed glasses. In his mouth is an unlighted Oppie-style pipe.)*

DICK. A lot of you freshmen – and I've always loved the freshman class best

(a rowdy response)

CLASS. We love you Dick!

DICK. Oh, yeah? Then why did you poke fun at my van?

CLASS. Because you got PHOTON license plates!

(laughter)

And your van's got Feynman diagrams all over it!

DICK. Why shouldn't I have Feynman diagrams all over it? I AM Richard Feynman!

(Cheers. A slide showing a photograph of Dick's van is projected on a screen.)

When you first come on campus and look at my van you see squiggly lines that don't mean anything to you. Well, by the time you graduate you're going to read my van! I got the Nobel Prize for those squiggles.

See, in a nutshell, the diagrams are a convenient language to make a lot of equations come together in one picture. It's tremendously liberating, you can do all kinds of things with them graphically combining many steps into one and go straight to the answer! You can translate a drawing into mathematics. I kind of reconstructed the whole of physics, getting precise measurements where before people got absurd answers. Listen, using my methods, if you measured the

DICK. *(cont.)* the distance from L.A. to New York it would be exact to the thickness of a human hair. How about that? That's how delicately I've checked out Quantum Electrodynamics. Gee, I never thought I was delicate about anything. Before I came along it was a very lengthy affair doing the numbers. So I got the Nobel Prize for that. You can get a Nobel Prize, too. All you've got to do is identify a problem and solve it – BAM! I love difficult problems. Problems are interesting. I've got a big personal problem to discuss with you in a minute – professional and personal – when I get up the courage to open up to you about it. Problems I like, honors I don't. My greatest fear about going to Sweden to accept the damn thing – and I almost didn't – my Pop's memory was holding me back – because he wouldn't have approved of me being beholden to aristocratic aims – a big show for the King – my Pop was a man of the people – didn't want me to be fooled by gold braid and other external signs of power, so my fear about showing up to the Nobel Prize ceremony was that I had to put on white tie and tails! Well, here's the scary part, I thought that you're not supposed to turn your back on the King when you pick up your award, you're supposed to back up the stairs. I was so afraid I was going to trip on my tails that I practiced hopping backwards in my hotel room.

(He hops backwards, falls on his ass. Is stunned for a second. The class gasps. A **BEAUTIFUL YOUNG COED** *– played by the actress who plays* **ARLENE** *– springs forward, helps him up. She wears a Caltech sweater.)*

Phooey! Thanks. I ain't dead yet. Don't sit down, Miss. I need your help.

(He takes out stack of photographs upside down from his briefcase.)

A lot of you young ladies sitting in the front here have been leaving pin-ups of yourselves with my secretary. I'm returning them to you today.

VOICES OF GIRLS. Oh, no. Phooey!

DICK. Although my eyesight ain't what it used to be – the eyes are the first to go – I can see you're all very beautiful in addition to being very brainy.

GIRLS. Keep them!

DICK. I want to clarify something about my physical condition. There's some speculation that I've got weird stomach cancers because I worked on the Atomic Bomb. But, I don't believe working on the Manhattan Project has anything to do with it. It's been a long while since then, and I've had a full life. Besides, I've always had a nervous tummy. When my folks came up to M.I.T. for my graduation I landed in the hospital for three days! Sure, my cancers are mysterious and I'm fighting them. But, it is true that being in danger makes me think about the people who came before.

(He stares at the **COED.***)*

COED. We love you, Dick.

DICK. Miss, could you please hand back these juicy pin-ups. I haven't looked at them. You'd do better, uh, getting to know some of the guys slouching in the back rows. It's very important for you all to live full lives. Have fun. I want you to realize that there's a lot of stuff can't be found in books, can't be measured or predicted – like love. It's the wackiest thing. Totally crazy. But what an elegant high. You're going to be studying high-energy physics. Well, how are you going to know, identify, the soaring sensation, the thrill, the scariness of…the unknown…if you don't let go and leap without a safety net? Courage is what it takes in the laboratory. And in life. Don't be lazy. Don't waste a minute of your time. Waitresses understand that. They don't waste a minute.. Had a waitress girl friend could turn over seven customers during lunchtime. Yeah, I'd say I've learned plenty from the ladies. My first wife, Arlene, got me to appreciate drawing. During the war, we wrote letters to each other in Chinese pictograms, to drive the censors crazy. That was when I was working on the atomic

DICK. *(cont.)* bomb. Hey, maybe that was the start of my diagrams....She died. Very young. Like the young teacher Christa McAuliffe, who was one of the brave young people on the Challenger Space Shuttle. I've been asked to join the commission of experts set up to find out what caused the fuel to leak, catch fire and explode. That means that I would have to get off my comfort zone here. With you. Leave.

CLASS. Phooey!

DICK. Gosh, I don't want to go. What should I do?

MAN. I got a lot riding on my education!

DICK. I decided a long time ago to honor the life of the mind, not be out there in the world. So, it's a big decision for me to venture out into hostile territory. Am I man enough to play hard ball with killers? In fact, I know the strain will cost me. I'm talking to you a little bit like a father today because I might not get another chance, if I go, I'll give the investigation every last breath of my existence. I mention this, not just to learn what you think, but, importantly, you, also, might find yourselves in this kind of stew – living the life of theoretical, abstract thinkers. Then, suddenly, the world intrudes.

Hell, it's a paradox, ain't it? We get into this to find out how the world works. But, we leave the world itself, in order to study it. Because I've been thinking about my parents, I've been thinking about yours. I'll bet they're asking, "Show me the application of all the abstract brainy stuff you're studying." Well, you might tell them that a lot of Einstein's work informs our daily lives, governing everything from the atomic bomb to a television cathode-ray tube to the carbon dating of prehistoric paintings. And I've explained a lot of physics in my time that makes the laser possible. You're going to be hearing a lot about lasers in years ahead. The laser beam is made of large numbers of concentrated light particles, or photons, all operating on the same frequency-like billions of voices singing perfectly as one. Well, it's up to the next guy to apply my scholarship. I guess what Washington wants is to use my brains to solve this awful tragedy. Bastards! Used Oppie's brains, then cut him off at the knees. Guess you read Oppie died.

VOICE. Who?

DICK. Washington cut him off at the knees.

*(**GWENYTH** enters wearing a blue bathing suit drying her hair. During the following, she lays the towel on the ground and takes a sunbath. **DICK** applies sun tan lotion to her body. She speaks with a British accent and is played by the same actress who plays **SALLY RAND**.)*

GWENYTH. Just think about those old farts in Washington in their droopy drawers And you won't be intimidated by them one bit.

DICK. My pop would have liked you.

GWENYTH. You're undressing me with your eyes, aren't you?

DICK. I'll never forget the first time I saw you coming out of Lake Geneva in your blue bathing suit, trembling, a raven-haired Venus. I thought I'd died and gone to heaven.

GWENYTH. But you don't believe in heaven.

DICK. The day my pop was buried, my Mom asked a Rabbi to say prayers. I really blew my stack. Pop didn't believe in religious rituals. Boy, I went wild. I defended Pop's life-long commitment to reason. What I wasn't understanding was how much my poppy loved my mom. So, he wouldn't have minded, if having a Rabbi on hand was a help to my mom with her grief. God, I was pissed off about a lot of things after the war. A real angry kid; I laid it all on my mom and the Rabbi. There isn't much I regret in my life, but my juvenile behavior that day…Gwenyth, I wish I could relive that day, Make it right. Clean up my act.

GWENYTH. I think I would have liked your father. He would have backed me up when you get intractable.

DICK. I been thinking a lot about what he'd say about me going to Washington. He had a scorn for guys in uniform, authority figures. It was bad enough that I accepted the Noble Prize. Pop just hated aristocracy, all that –

GWENYTH. He would have loved the trumpets, don't you think?

DICK. No trumpets in D.C.

GWENYTH. But lots of fanfare. It's going to be a public relations circus.What a chance for you to prick all the hot-air posturing that's going to be done before the press. You could really deflate their phony rhetoric. I think that would please your father very much.

DICK. I'm of two minds about the whole thing: I can't do anything in a half-assed way, so I'd throw myself into the investigation all stops out. But the price is steep. I ain't got a lot of energy to spare, sweetheart.

GWENYTH. Maybe your body is slowing down, but, baby, your brain is not. Your adorable brain.

(He laughs.)

DICK. Boy, if I had known at the start that dames dug brains, I wouldn't have worried so much about my klutzy athletic coordination. Phooey.

GWENYTH. When we met in Geneva and you told me you were attending a world-class scientific conference, I became intrigued right away.

DICK. And I was so worried that sex and science don't mix. *Now*, I get it when...

GWENYTH. When what?

DICK. When it's all coming to an end.

GWENYTH. The brave people on the Challenger were too young to die, sweetness. And, I suspect their deaths could have been prevented. I'm sure it hasn't escaped you that on board was a young woman –

DICK. Christa MacCullough, the schoolteacher from New England. President Reagan was supposed to receive a phone call from space from her during his State of the Union address. The Shuttle had to be launched fast, ready or not. I think her voice was also scheduled to be piped into classrooms all over the globe. She was too young to die.

GWENYTH. Surely, you made a mental connection between that girl and Arlene?

DICK. And me. Because she was a teacher, too. My sister could have been on board. She always wanted to conquer space travel.

GWENYTH. Spot-on! You were born to be on the Challenger Commisssion. You have the research skills and the teaching ability to explain your highly technical findings in simple language. This final, great accomplishment could be the jewel in your crown.

DICK. You're so British. My Britannica.

GWENYTH. You're not dead yet, darling.

(She grabs his behind.)

It will do you good to get out off your comfort zone and fight the good fight. I've never regretted for one instant that I flew away from everything I hold dear to venture into a foreign world full of physicists.

DICK. Gee, I never felt foreign.

GWENYTH. Do you consider yourself normal?

DICK. Well, I'm not lazy.

GWENYTH. That's true.

DICK. Neither are you.

GWENYTH. We make a good couple.

DICK. A couple of what?

(They laugh.)

GWENYTH. What would happen if we changed places?

DICK. You mean what would happen if I could be you and you could be me? Hmmm…

GWENYTH. I'm serious.

DICK. You're not talking about costumes?

GWENYTH. We could go as each other to the next faculty fancy dress ball. Hmmm…

DICK. The hell with a fantasy bash, you could go in my place to testify in Washington, D.C.

GWENYTH. Right-oh. I'd be happy to go, if it would give you a few more months of life.

(She does her Richard Feynman imitation.)

Mr. Friggin' Chairman and youse big-time asstronuts and stuffed shoit generals on de panel – I gotta tell youse, I broke my policy to stay outta Washington because my old man brought me up ta give de bad guys de finger. And I'm here ta tell ya dat I done my homewoik. In case you're wonderin' what I been doin' while de rest of youse was takin' public relations tours ta Cape Canaveral, I was talkin' to de blue collar types dat did de actual building of de Shuttle, were right der when it was assembled on de launchin' pad on dat dark and cold mornin'. Puttin' together what de engineers told me at de Jet Propulsion Laboratory in Pasadena where my sister woiks, matchin' up de manufacturer's tests results and de real thing in action.

*(***DICK*** is delighted.)*

DICK. Spot-on!

(He kisses her.)

So, what's really bugging you?

GWENYTH. Your faithful secretary, Penelope, called me to say you returned a stack of pin-up photos to this year's crop of nubile coeds. She was worried, thought you must really be under the weather to take such drastic, old-foggy action. One of the advantages of teaching in California is the health of the young women about.

DICK. I ain't an old foggy.

GWENYTH. No, indeed. I was just concerned that your medical condition had broken your spirit. That's why I think you should go to Washington. I hope your

famous curiosity is wet. I'm going to call your sister.
She'll help you.

(During the following. the lights change as **DICK** *begins
to speak his thoughts to the Challenger Inquiry Commission in Washington, D.C. A long table, chair, and table
microphone materialize.)*

DICK. When we were kids, we were so hopeful in science
and technology, busting to make life better for everybody. And it has, when discoveries are converted into
practical, affordable fun gadgets. But we always get
into terrible trouble when we go to the very edge of
things and don't test stuff properly. People die in the
process. The cost is so great. Once upon a time – the
scientific community was so small...checks and bal-
ances were automatic. We welcomed scrutiny, didn't
fear informed criticism, we were open, about everything, that's the point of scientific method, isn't it?
Progress comes from making your findings public, so
another guy can build on your work, make the world a
better place. That's the point isn't?

But then, the government got involved. And a veil of
secrecy was drawn over all our laboratories. And with
good reason. We were at war. All our brainpower was
aimed toward destruction. And we won the war. Suddenly, science became big business. Huge grants to
universities to build expensive cyclotrons, new build-
ings, and we physicists became bigger than Groucho,
Jack, and Fred, Hollywood stars. We picked up Nobel
Prizes along the way. None of us can live up to the
expectations of the public. It's crazy. What happened?

*(The room begins to hush, as the audience starts to listen
to him.)*

Folks, I just want you to know where I'm coming from.
I truly grieve for the entire crew of the Challenger. But
my heart breaks particularly for that girl, the teacher
from somewhere in New England, the McAulliffe girl.
See, if we don't respect life in this country, we're...just...
lost. That puff of smoke...the flames shooting up...

(There is an uncomfortable hush.)

CHAIRMAN. Dr. Feynman...your microphone is on...

DICK. Oh, yeah?

CHAIRMAN. You must have pushed the button accidentally.

DICK. Sorry. I'm a klutz when it comes to mechanical stuff.

CHAIRMAN. Professor Feynman isn't himself. He's under the weather. Sir, please sit. Rest your bones.

DICK. All my life people have been telling me to shut up and sit down.

CHAIRMAN. The button!

DICK. Oh! Can I make one request before I turn the damn thing off?

CHAIRMAN. Certainly. But make it quick. You've already disrupted the proper order of our proceedings. I know you don't mean to.

DICK. I gotta have a tall glass of ice water.

CHAIRMAN. Could we have ice water for *all* the participants, please.

DICK. That's going to take more time!

*(***DICK*** *begins drumming on the table.)*

CHAIRMAN. Before we begin, I want to reiterate to Congress, the press, and the grieving families, that we are not conducting this investigation in a manner which would be unfairly critical of NASA, because we think – I certainly think – NASA has done an excellent job, and I think the American people do. Dr, Feynman, could you please stop drumming.

DICK. Sorry.

CHAIRMAN. President Ronald Reagan, who is determined to continue support of the space program, appointed this investigatory commission. And by the end of the day, we will conclude our findings. Just a few more witnesses and the conclusions of some members of this commission. I call on Mr. Graham, acting administrator of space.

*(**GRAHAM** appears in his own light. he is played by the actor who played Franky, the motorcycle cop.)*

GRAHAM. In the interest of total disclosure – Thirty years ago I sat in a class called Phyiscs Ten. It was the best course at Caltech. It was taught by that gentleman, sitting there, Dr. Richard Feynman. His methods were unique. Unorthodox, to say the least. But to this day, I recall practically every principle he taught us. Particle science has never been the same following his work because –

CHAIRMAN. Mr. Graham, our time is limited. Dr. Feynman's achievements are spelled out in the press kit.

DICK. Hi, Graham.

GRAHAM. The nation is grateful that you are allowing us to use the very short time you've got left.

DICK. I ain't dead yet.

*(**JULIUS** enters, whispers to **CHAIRMAN**, who uses a gavel.)*

CHAIRMAN. Dr. Feynman, you are excused. A plane, equipped with a hospital bed and staffed with medical personnel, is fueled and ready to fly you home immediately.

DICK. I'll be as quick and clear as I can be. From the moment I was appointed to this commission, I started digging. Met with a series of engineers at the Jet Propulsion Laboratory in Pasadena. My sister works there. So, I turned to them with confidence because they'd worked on solid rocket boosters and the engines. From the first day we noted well-known problems with the rubber O-rings....

*(**JULIUS** moves away quickly.)*

...that sealed the joints between sections of the tall solid-fuel rockets. Ordinary rubber rings. Hey, what happened to my microphone? What the hell, I'm used to addressing a lecture hall full of people.

(He stands.)

Can you hear me back there?

VOICES. Yes.

DICK. Sir, can we talk about the weather? No one has so far.

CHAIRMAN. Who can stop you?

DICK. The day of the launch, it was so cold ice formed on the equipment all over the launching pad. Graham, did you get any warning that low temperature could pose a problem?

CHAIRMAN. If talk about the weather had been of significance, it would have been introduced as a fruitful topic before now, by more knowledgeable experts in the field of aerodynamics.

GRAHAM. I wish to answer the question now. The night before the launch, there was a discussion with the manufacturer about the O-rings. Low temperatures was a concern. A representative of the company, Mr. Lowenthal, is standing right there. Didn't you recommend that the launch proceed?

JULIUS. That is correct.

CHAIRMAN. There, Dr. Feynman. Are you satsfied?

DICK. Hey, Julius. Wasn't there evidence of "blow-by"?

CHAIRMAN. What is that? What is the significance of that?

JULIUS. Blow-by is soot.

DICK. There was evidence of soot showing that hot gases had burned through seals that were supposed to contain them. We're here to learn if that's significant or not.

CHAIRMAN. Go home, Dr. Feynman. You mustn't strain yourself. Lowenthal, would you please escort Dr. Feynman to his flight?

JULIUS. Of course.

(He steps forward.)

But I'd like to emphasize that the O-rings were used in pairs. And that the secondary O-rings always seemed to hold.

CHAIRMAN. That wasn't any cause for concern, was it?

GRAHAM. Oh, yes. That is an anomaly.

(a stirring of the audience)

Isn't that so, Mr. Lowenthal?

JULIUS. I feel a bit caught off guard. Mr. Graham's agency knew all along of a potential loss of resiliency when the rubber O-rings were cold. Come on, Feynman, let's scram.

DICK. I'm sick. I'm sweating. I gotta have a glass of ice water fast. Or I ain't moving. Boy, it's like pulling teeth around here getting the most simple stuff.

CHAIRMAN. Mr. Lowenthal, would you be so kind to see to it, so we can bring the proceedings back to a semblance of order.

JULIUS. Yes, Sir.

(He goes.)

CHAIRMAN. Before the assembly weighs Dr. Feynman's words, it is important to clarify that he is taking strong medication, due to a serious illness.

DICK. Just one more question. Graham, would you tell us please why resiliency was crucial?

GRAHAM. Because a soft metal-like lead, squeezed into a gap would not be able to hold a seal amid the vibration and changing pressure.

DICK. If this material weren't resilient for say a second or two, that would be enough to be a very dangerous situation, wouldn't it? I've got to tell you, I've been very frustrated by the documents I requested, which show how the rubber responded over a period of hours – instead of milliseconds. Why can't the space agency answer a simple question?

GRAHAM. Because a straight-forward test has never been performed.

*(**PEOPLE** in the room are stunned.)*

DICK. *(quietly)* Then perhaps we can perform one now.

CHAIRMAN. Now?

DICK. I'm prepared to do just that – perform for you a little experiment.

CHAIRMAN. Here?

DICK. Here.

CHAIRMAN. This is not a laboratory. The conditions…are not scientific.

DICK. They are. As any child knows, transformations can be achieved without spending a lot of money.

(pulls out pliers and a small C clamp)

These pliers didn't cost me an arm and a leg. This little C clamp a few pennies more. Just a couple of simple everyday objects are needed. Toys, really. It's the scientific principle that counts. Where's my water?

Could I take a look at the model of the Space Shuttle, please?

CHAIRMAN. Bring Dr. Feynman the Challenger model.

VOICES. The model of the Challenger…the model…. bring…what? The what?

DICK. *(calling)* The coffin! Bring the model of the billion-dollar coffin!

Mr. Chairman, I've got to attend a funeral, so I'll be outta your hair pretty soon.

(The tall model of the Challenger is placed on the table in front of DICK, who addresses GRAHAM.)

This reproduces the materials used?

GRAHAM. It does.

DICK. I'm going to take out a section of the rubber O-rings.

GRAHAM. Do it.

DICK. I'm sweating, I can't see straight.

(DICK takes out a handkerchief, wipes his glasses. Using his pliers, removes rubber from the model. JULIUS brings DICK a glass of ice water.)

JULIUS. Your ice water.

DICK. Oh, boy! Thanks, brother. I'm ready. Mr. Chairman, I'll say my piece and get out of here.

CHAIRMAN. I grant you the floor for five minutes.

DICK. See, I've taken a section of the rubber O-ring material from the model. It springs back and forth. Now, I'm going to put it in this ice water. Ice is a stable 32 degrees. The exact temperature at the time of the launch.The shuttle's solid rocket boosters were made in sections, assembled one atop another at the launch site. The joints holding the sections together had to be sealed to prevent the escape of hot gases from inside the rocket. The pressure of the gas was supposed to wedge them tightly into the joints, creating the seal. Okay, now, I'm taking this stuff that I got out of your seal and putting into the ice water.

(to himself, while he waits:)

I wonder why? I wonder why? I wonder why I wonder Now I take it out and I put some pressure on it .

(He folds cold rubber into a C clamp, tightens the screw.)

Now I undo it. What do we discover? It doesn't stretch back. It stays the same dimension. In other words, for a few seconds at least and more than that, there is no resilience in this particular material when it is at a temperature of 32 degrees. I believe that has some significance for our problem. Nature cannot be fooled.

(A moment of silence. Then, a burst of **VOICES***, flash bulbs.* **DICK** *stands, exhausted, removes his glasses.* **CHAIRMAN** *bangs his gavel.)*

CHAIRMAN. Silence!

REPORTER. Then those people died because of beaurocratic negligence!

CHAIRMAN. This is merely a minority report!

REPORTER. A statement, please, Dr. Feynman.

CHAIRMAN. Things are getting out of control here! Clear the room.

DICK. For a successful technology, reality must take precedence over public relations. I gotta go to Poppy's funeral.

REPORTER. Dr. Feynman, you singled out Christy McAulliffe. Why?

DICK. Because she wanted to teach kids how beautiful the world is.

(He collapses.)

VOICES. Feynman's down! Call the medics!

(A grown up JOAN appears to DICK, takes his arm.)

JOAN. Let's go home.

CHAIRMAN. Clear the room! Clear the room!

DICK. I'm so proud of you.

JOAN. Thank you for giving me half of the universe.

DICK. I know you are making good use of it.

(In DICK's mind, he's back in Far Rockaway. Fall, 1946.)

LUCILLE. Thank God you're home. You were born to bury your father. Good news! Your father's going to be buried next to your brother.

(She carries a suit, tie, polished shoes.)

Mel is going to have a proper funeral today.

JOAN. I'll go make sandwiches.

(She goes. DICK sits, plays his bongos.)

LUCILLE. What are you doing?

DICK. I'm not talkin' ta ya.

LUCILLE. Put aside those bongos, you aren't a boy any more.

DICK. I'm writing a letter to Arlene. In my head. I wanna tell her I got a teaching job.

LUCILLE. Here. Put on your father's inheritance. You get all his clothes.

DICK. No.

LUCILLE. You look like a bum. Respect his memory. He may have been an atheist, but he was a sharp dresser. True or false?

DICK. Oh, the hell with it.

LUCILLE. He knew, he knew the secret of the universe – How to make a woman happy. He was a god when it came to –

DICK. Great men know my name. But around here I'm a bum. Why is that?

LUCILLE. Wait till you kids see the family mausoleum my father made for us in Queens. The Russians are never going to break in. Once we're dead, honey, we'll all be safe. Be a nice boy and offer to address Rabbi Cahn's congregation about the Atomic Bomb.

DICK. MA!

LUCILLE. He's very up-to-date. So good-looking.

DICK. Call off the Rabbi!

LUCILLE. Uncle Sam would have made a man of you. It would have been better for you to come out of the trenches wearing a Chaplain's uniform like Rabbi Cahn. What a man!

DICK. Pop hated guys in uniform.

LUCILLE. So, are you ready to rise to the occasion?

(We are at Bayside Cemetery, Queens. JOAN stands next to DICK.)

JOAN. Hey, Brother, what does this stone pile remind you of?

DICK. A bomb shelter.

JOAN. Exactly.

LUCILLE. Shhh – the coffin.

(RABBI CAHN appears. He is played by the same actor who played MEL. He wears his handsome Army Chaplain uniform.)

DICK. *(He stares.)* You're....

LUCILLE. *(to DICK)* Respect.

RABBI. Let's begin. Richard, recite Kaddish with me.

DICK. My father was a scientist.

RABBI. *(to* **LUCILLE***)* I thought you said he sold uniforms?

DICK. No disrespect, Rabbi, but my father stood for skepticism, not superstition.

(**LUCILLE** *kicks him.*)

LUCILLE. No "isms" in the cemetery.

DICK. I don't know Hebrew.

RABBI. Let's say the Mourners Prayer in English.

DICK. I'm going to blow my stack.

LUCILLE. I like it better in Hebrew.

RABBI. Me, too.

LUCILLE. More eternal.

DICK. This stinks to high heaven. Crazy.

JOAN. Can't you both see he's broken-hearted?

DICK. I'm goin' ta blow, I'm goin' ta blow.

LUCILLE. Start Rabbi, in Hebrew, he'll follow the bouncing ball.

JOAN. Rabbi, my brother's had to sign *two* death certificates lately. Another death opens the wounds of the first one. And he hasn't been able to mourn her properly. None of us has.

RABBI. Why wasn't I told? You just had another funeral?

DICK. My wife.

RABBI. Did I meet her?

DICK. We were married by a judge.

LUCILLE. It was a love marriage. They lived in Albuquerque.

RABBI. What were you doing out there?

(silence)

DICK. Putzie was in a Presbyterian sanatorium.

LUCILLE. When you wrote Putzie missed her period –

RABBI. – The coffin –

DICK. – That proved to be only a symptom of her illness.

RABBI. Was she Presbyterian?

LUCILLE. Well, she came from Cederhurst. Arlene Greenbaum. But Richard called her Putzie.

RABBI. Oh.

DICK. And she called me Coach.

JOAN. I loved her.

LUCILLE. Rabbi, if it's all right by you, can we remember Mrs. Richard Feynman today, too.

JOAN. Two for the price of one.

LUCILLE. Sister!

JOAN. Sorry.

DICK. Ma, thanks for callin' Putzie Mrs. Feynman.

LUCILLE. Maybe she was your wife, Ritty, but she became my sick daughter.

JOAN. My big sister.

LUCILLE. She should have been buried here.

DICK. Yeah, but her folks wanted her coffin. So, I caved in.

LUCILLE. You shouldn't have.

DICK. I thought you didn't want her.

LUCILLE. I wanted her.

DICK. Rabbi, can I go get her?

RABBI. Not today. Okay. I'm going to pray.

LUCILLE. Wait. Rabbi, I want us to include the Japanese in this.

RABBI. What Japanese?

LUCILLE. The ones my son, the physicist, murdered.

RABBI. During the war?

LUCILLE. Thousands.

JOAN. Ritty, don't cave in any more.

DICK. Okay.

JOAN. About anything.

DICK. I DIDN'T KILL THOUSANDS OF JAPANESE.

LUCILLE. Where are HIROSHIMA and NAGASAKI today?

DICK. In fact, when I heard the news, I vomited in the bushes. We wanted to give Hitler the finger. We never imagined our baby would be dropped on innocent civilians.

JOAN. Stop carrying the weight of the world on your back.

DICK. How can I do that?

JOAN. Have fun.

LUCILLE. We used to have fun. It's my fault. For whatever I've done, I'll spend what's left of my life trying.... trying to make up for...The problem, believe it or not, is just that the Feynmans...we love too much.

DICK. It's a problem.

LUCILLE. So you agree?

> (*DICK* nods. **LUCILLE** *gathers her* **CHILDREN** *in her arms.*)

RABBI. You have very modern children, Mrs. Feynman. That's a blessing. Both beautiful. It's encouraging to me to know that there are young American Jews who will insure our future. They've got backbone. We need to inform, revitalize our beliefs. Test them.

DICK. Death is so final. I'm burned out, Rabbi. I haven't an idea in my head.

RABBI. Well, it takes a woman to get our blood boiling, doesn't it? Flowing to our brains.

DICK. A dirty-minded Rabbi! Hallelujah! My Pop would've liked you.

RABBI. Remember, I've just spent a couple of years with young guys like you as a Chaplain under fire. Richard, you are a lover. I'll bet women fall all over themselves for you.

DICK. My father believed sex and science don't mix.

RABBI. *My* father feels sex and spirituality don't mix. But, there's a science to it.

DICK. I gotta catch a train.

> (*The* **RABBI** *begins to pray.*)

RABBI. Today, we mourn Melville Feynman, the scientist. Arlene Greenbaum Feynman, beloved wife of Richard, and the people of Hiroshima and Nagasaki.

(While Kaddish is being said quietly, DICK *arrives in a park at Cornell University. It is fall and a few golden leaves drop from the trees.)*

Yit-ga-dal ve-yit-ka-dash she-mei ra-ba be-al-ma di-ve-ra chi-re-u-tei, ve-yam-lich mal-chu-tei be-cha-yei-chon u-veyo-mei-chon u-ve-cha-yei de-chol beit/ Yis-ra-eil, ba-a-ga la u-vi-ze-man kariv, ve-i-me-ru: a-mein.

(As DICK *looks up and speaks, the entire cast begins to appear in silhouette, holding leaves in their hands.)*

DICK. Putzie, although you've been dead for two years, I want you to know that I got a teaching job here at Cornell. Frankly, I don't have the heart to start teaching. I came a couple of days early to case out the joint. So what happened? There are still war time housing shortages around here. There ain't a bed to be had anywhere. So, I'm making a bed for myself outta dead leaves.

(He gets on the ground, starts to put leaves over himself.)

I thought you'd be glad I got a teaching job, so I'm telling you. I miss you. Good night.

(He lies back, sleeps. GWENYTH, *wearing a mourning veil, along with the other cast members, lets the leaves in her hand fall. The campus bell strikes one as...)*

(THE CURTAIN FALLS.)

ABOUT THE AUTHOR

ARTHUR GIRON's latest play is *St. Francis in Egypt,* and he is co-writing the book for a musical *Amazing Grace.* He was named "one of the best contemporary dramatists" by critic Rosette LaMont. His plays are performed continuously throughout the country. *Becoming Memories* (published by Samuel French) won a Los Angeles Critics Drama-Logue Award for "Outstanding Achievement in Writing." It has been seen in over 70 cities. *The New York Times* described his play Edith Stein (also published by Samuel French) as being "filled with passionate ideas." It will be seen in Buenos Aires. His play *Flight* (published by Samuel French) toured 120 cities. He is a founding member of the Ensemble Studio Theatre, which produced his plays *Moving Bodies* (published by Samuel French), *Innocent Pleasures,* and *Boys Dies Dancing Mambo* (Money). Other plays include *The Coffee Trees, A Dream of Wealth, Charley Bacon and His Family, Scouts Honor* (Dirty Jokes) and *Emilie's Voltaire,* which was awarded the Galileo Prize.

Also by
Arthur Giron...

Becoming Memories

Edith Stein

Flight

Emilie's Voltaire

OTHER TITLES AVAILABLE FROM SAMUEL FRENCH

EMILIE'S VOLTAIRE

Arthur Giron

Dramatic Comedy / 1m, 1f / Simple Set

Emilie's Voltaire is a passionate comic-drama that explores a love affair that scandalized all of Europe between Voltaire, the greatest wit of his time, and the beautiful scientist Emilie du Chatelet. It takes place before the French Revolution.

Winner of the Galileo Prize

"What happens when the minds of two seekers of knowledge, one a challenger of life and the other a hedonistic rule breaker, meet? The result is a tumultuous, fascinating 16-year love affair that is wonderfully portrayed in Arthur Giron's *Emilie's Voltaire*...The captivating *Emilie's Voltaire* is an inside look at genius and the underlying emotions that feed it. Definitely a bit of history you're pleased to discover."
–OffBroadway.com

"The intellectual, emotional and sexual sparks fly...an unusual and fascinating play."
– William Wolf, *Wolf Entertainment Guide*

"Arthur Giron's words are what actors long to wrap their voices around."
– *The New York Examiner*

"A beautiful pas de deux of dialogue!"
–MusicOMH

OTHER TITLES AVAILABLE FROM SAMUEL FRENCH

THE FARNSWORTH INVENTION

Aaron Sorkin

Drama / 15m, 3f

It's 1929. Two ambitious visionaries race against each other to invent a device called "television." Separated by two thousand miles, each knows that if he stops working, even for a moment, the other will gain the edge. Who will unlock the key to the greatest innovation of the 20th century: the ruthless media mogul, or the self-taught Idaho farm boy?

The answer comes to compelling life in *The Farnsworth Invention*, the new play from Aaron Sorkin, creator of *The West Wing*.

"...vintage Sorkin and crackling prime-time theater...breezy and shrewd, smart-alecky and idealistic."
- Newsday

"...a firecracker of a play in a fittingly snap, crackle and pop production under the direction of Des McAnuff, the drama has among its many virtues the ability to make you think at the same time that it breaks your heart."
- Chicago Sun-Times

"The most exciting new play on Broadway...a rousing theatrical experience."
- MTV News